Boy Toy

(Book Two of the Confessions of a Chick Magnet series)

by Jenny Gardiner

What people are saying about Jenny Gardiner's books:

Red Hot Romeo
"Awesome". So enjoyed the romantic chemistry between the two characters. Read it non stop into the wee hours. Highly recommend this book
-- Mrs. K

Blue-Blooded Romeo
"Another brilliant, fun read from Jenny Gardiner. The book is fun to read and I thoroughly enjoyed every word. Jenny Gardiner has put the fun back into romance books and I look forward to each book in this delightful series."
-- Anne Blyth

"I had planned on only reading a few chapters at first but couldn't put it down. A terrific storyline, well-developed and extremely relatable characters, what's not to love?? Great read!"
-- Samantha Reeves

Big O Romeo
"I could not put this book down. Warning don't start this book late at night as you will not want to stop reading.
-- Di

Sleeping with Ward Cleaver

"A fun, sassy read! A cross between Erma Bombeck and Candace Bushnell, reading Jenny Gardiner is like sinking your teeth into a chocolate cupcake…you just want more."

--Meg Cabot, NY Times bestselling author of Princess Diaries, Queen of Babble and more

Slim to None

"Jenny Gardiner has done it again--this fun, fast-paced book is a great summer read."

--Sarah Pekkanen, NY Times bestselling author of *The Opposite of Me*

Chapter One

SULLIVAN Forester stood before his open underwear drawer, and for what seemed like the thousandth time over the past year, he stared at the black velvet box nestled beneath a stack of boxers, topped by the pair with Saint Bernards embroidered on them. He shook his head, smacked his lips, then ran his fingers through his wavy caramel hair, which was a little longer than he liked it of late. At last, he took a deep breath and blew it out, deciding once and for all to make it official. Today was the day he was going to start getting his shit together, which included trimming this shaggy head of hair.

But first, he had more important business to attend to: the ring.

He pulled the box out of the drawer where it had lurked, taunting him for what seemed like ages now, and flipped open the lid to stare at the Tiffany & Co. two-carat brilliant-cut diamond engagement ring, flanked on either side by fat indigo sapphires. The gems caught the early morning sunlight streaming through the window and winked at him. He took it as yet one more sign that it was time to find a new home for this thing that felt like bad juju now that it had taken up unproductive space in his life for far too long.

At first, when Gretchen Penobscott dumped him, three whoppingly inconsiderate weeks before their wedding, it seemed like he would never get over it. Why would she do something like that to him? Worse still, how could he have been so clueless and not seen it coming?

A year ago, her words lacerated his heart, causing an achy tug that didn't let up for months.

"Look, Sully," she'd said. "I've realized marriage isn't for me."

He remembered staring into her brown eyes, the ones that once seemed so warm and loving, finally seeing them for the cold dark they had been all along. Her shiny black hair was pulled back into a high ponytail, her makeup fresh. She wore one of her never-ending supply of bright pastel sundresses—what were they called? Lilly something or other. He knew dick about fashion, but he always noticed she was about the only woman in town who dressed every day as if she was going to a cocktail party at a beach resort. He knew that style of dress only because it was emblematic of what he'd left behind after moving to Bristol, Montana a handful of years ago. That's when he'd sold his start-up for more money than he could ever envision in his bank account.

He'd spent a couple of years dabbling in the lavish me-me-me lifestyle of the wealthy in New York: the obligatory summers in the Hamptons, the mandatory charity events every night of the week at somebody-or-other's exclusive penthouse apartment during the rest of the year. The insincere air-kiss greetings by women who wanted your donations but not a decent conversation, the severe handshakes by the Wall Street assholes who were dipping into the cash reserves of the country to line their own pockets all while sticking their dicks into women young enough to be their daughters, as their air kissing wives went under the knife for yet more unnecessary plastic surgery to try desperately to compete.

Sully was over that bullshit, which was why he'd come to Bristol. He wanted to start new where no one knew him, where he could be his authentic self and not play the superficial games to which he'd become accustomed.

His mistake, however, was bringing Gretchen Penobscott with him. He and Gretchen had been together even during the leaner years, so at least he could take comfort knowing it wasn't as if she'd been after his wealth. And to her credit, for a while, she went along with his plan, upending the lifestyle she'd become quite accustomed to. She came with him to Montana, Lilly whatever-the-name-was dresses and all, but it seemed from the minute they'd moved here, things were never quite the same between them.

He'd hoped it was only a matter of getting used to things—it was admittedly weird going from endless black pavement and skyscrapers to fields of wildflowers and mountains that touched the skies instead—and that once married she'd settle in more. But then he never got the chance to see if he was right because on that brutal early summer day a year ago, she slid the ring off her left ring finger, tucked it into the palm of his hand, closing his fingers around it, gave him a chaste kiss on the cheek, and walked away.

Well. He eventually learned that time does heal old wounds, and though he'd once loved Gretchen, she'd done him a solid by not going through with what she knew in her heart would be a mistake. He'd never fully understand it, but hey, much better than finding that out after the wedding. Sure, it sucked, worse still having to take the financial hit for canceling everything wedding-related at the last minute. But it hadn't even put a dent in his bank account, so calling it off may have cost him emotionally, but the lesson learned was not financially devastating.

And today, he was going to take the first step toward making some other person who couldn't afford it that much happier.

He whistled for his husky pup Blizzard, threw on a pair of shorts, a T-shirt, and a plaid flannel shirt to fend off the morning chill, grabbed his laptop, and went out on the deck off his bedroom. The sun was shining and the fog had begun to lift off the still snowcapped mountain peaks as he fixed a quick cappuccino at the coffee bar on his deck. He sat down at the long farmhouse table and opened his laptop, then snapped a quick picture of the ring on his phone, clicked on Facebook, and entered this:

Looking for a good home for this briefly used treasure, valued at $85,000. Tell me why you want to share this with the one you love. Please email me at sully@sullyforester.com. Deadline is one week from today. Please share.

He uploaded the image, clicked Post, and sent it off into the ether, then did the same on Twitter and Instagram. He rubbed his hands together, took a sip of his cappuccino, and made a mental note to remember to stop in at Jackson's Barber Shop for a haircut when he went to town later in the day.

Sully, who'd been working on writing a song, reveled in the beautiful weather. It had started out chilly, but by lunchtime, it was the quintessential Montana summer day: songbirds in full throat, the hum of bees vibrating through the air, all against the backdrop of a bluebird sky.

Wildflowers bloomed like crazy in the fields surrounding his custom-built farmhouse that overlooked the Rocky Mountains. The place was truly a slice of heaven.

Life could not be any better. Sure, Sully didn't have a bride at his side as he'd originally expected, but it was all good. He'd landed some regular gigs playing guitar at local bars, and making others happy with his music made him supremely happy. He had a great dog whose antics made him laugh. He got to spend time each morning doing what he wanted: reading, meditating, working out at the gym. He volunteered with an animal rescue clinic, thanks to his friend Tanner Eliasson, a local veterinarian. He even spent an inordinate amount of time cooking elaborate meals for himself each night, which was admittedly a little lonely, and occasionally hosted dinners with a handful of folks who'd become true friends unlike the superficial acquaintances he'd encountered regularly back on the East Coast.

Not to take dig at the East Coast—there was nothing wrong with that lifestyle for someone else, but it wasn't for him. He was happy on his horse or feeding his chickens or taking a hike on his hundred acres of property. And more than happy to not have to deal with rush hour traffic and type A personalities ever again.

His phone buzzed and he pulled up a text message from his friend Tanner:

Dude. What the fuck? Have you looked at your Facebook in the past hour?

Sully squinted, not knowing what exactly he was talking about. Until he remembered.

Oh, that. You saw it?

He waited for the buzz of his phone.

Saw it? Me and a few thousand other complete strangers.

9

Sully's eyes opened wide. Huh?

You're joking, right?

Tanner didn't comment but instead sent a screenshot of his post.

Sully expanded the image to see details up close. Well, crap. He grabbed his phone and pressed Tanner's number.

"Jesus, Sully," Tanner said. "Next time give me heads-up on these things. I've had every female I know within two hundred miles message me about this including my girlfriend, and I didn't even know about it. You're *giving* away that ring?"

"I figured it was time. The thing was taking up space, reminding me of what was. No need in going there anymore. I'm finally past Gretchen, over that whole breakup, and I want to make something that left a bad taste in my mouth become something better. Lemons to lemonade."

"That's a hell of a glass of lemonade," Tanner said.

"Yeah well, I thought it could be a fun project. And it would feel good helping someone else out who maybe couldn't afford to get engaged."

"Your fun project might turn into a full-time job if my suspicions are right—you'll be slammed with people begging for that thing."

Sully shrugged. "Great! The good news is I've got time to do what I want. And right now, this feels right. Besides, I'm sure I'll be able to see through the scammers looking for an expensive ring they could hock and find someone who is truly in love and has a legit reason for wanting this thing. And to be honest, the sooner I get rid of this, the better. I want to move on without any reminders."

"Yeah, well, you'd better open up that laptop and start reading your emails because I think you've given yourself a full-time unpaid job for the next year."

Sully laughed. "No worries. It's all good."

"Talk to me about 'all good' when you have a million women pounding your door down because they think you're the swooniest guy on the planet."

Huh. Sully hadn't thought about that. Shit. He sure as hell wasn't looking for women to glom onto him for his money. Over the last year since Gretchen had left, Sully had been in the habit of one-off flings with women tourists who streamed through Bristol like a hard-running river, looking for sporty outdoors activities by day and even more sporty activities in the sack by night.

His music gigs offered the perfect opportunity to meet strangers in town for a short period, guaranteeing he could avoid anyone seeking commitment or anything more than a few hours of escapist sex. He'd usually return with them to their hotel or Airbnb or rental up on the mountain, only to slip out hours later under cover of darkness and be back in his own bed before sunrise. Sure it seemed impersonal, but that's what he'd needed at the time—anonymous sex for the sake of sex, no strings attached, no commitment whatsoever.

But now, crap, did this mean women were going to seek him out? He hadn't thought about that. He should've donated the damned ring to charity to be done with it. Because the last thing he needed in his life was to have women homing in on him like a heat-seeking missile, wanting love and marriage and all those things he'd grown a bit cynical about.

He opened his Facebook page and saw that his post had been viewed by three thousand people and over four hundred people had commented. Hell, another two thousand had shared it. Ho-ly shit.

What had he gotten himself into?

Chapter Two

ISABELLE Strong was tired of licking her wounds over her latest failed relationship. Granted the hot guy from HR, her last impetuous fling, was never truly going to be long-term material—first off, nothing good came from dating a guy from the office. Second, it turned out he wasn't all that interesting. Once they got past the great sex—the only reason the relationship lasted as long as it did—she found herself carrying most conversations while he spent an inordinate amount of time on his phone's ESPN app. If he was going to be so deeply entrenched in his handheld idiot device this early into a relationship, Lord only knew how bad it would be after a few years together.

So she did what she knew she had to do and lowered the boom, dumping HR-boy before things got any more involved. And now she didn't miss him so much as the idea of him. Rather, the idea of a guy she could have fun with. Someone who could go away with her for the weekend, stay in to cook dinner, and maybe binge-watch several episodes of a Netflix show before retiring for a night of stimulating sex, ultimately falling asleep curled up in each other's arms. Was that so much to ask for?

Apparently so. Because she'd had a succession of equally lame relationships over the past few years—from the lifeguard in Santa Monica whose idea of a good time was watching shark documentaries, to the waiter at the Ivy who only cared which celebrity he'd waited on that week. She had to lose him because she couldn't bear to hear one more time about how he'd yet again served lunch to one of the Kardashians. Then there was the weird guy who had the creepy toe fetish and insisted she wear sandals even when they went to Banff for the weekend to ski. In the winter.

Uh, no.

She was stuck in traffic on the freeway and switched off her book on tape and turned up the radio to try to find out what was causing the logjam this time on the highway. Instead she got the tail end of a news report about some guy who'd posted on Facebook about giving away a ridiculously expensive engagement ring to a deserving person and that social networking sites had exploded over it.

Huh. Intriguing. What sort of guy would have bought an $85,000 engagement ring in the first place? And what self-respecting woman would ditch the kind of guy who did? Not that she was chasing after guys with money, but seriously, that woman must've been an idiot.

"The man, who lives in Bristol, Montana," the reporter said, "is taking pleas from hopeful suitors until the end of the week."

Bristol, Montana? That was where her best friend Zoey Richards had moved after falling in love with a gorgeous veterinarian. She wondered if Zoey knew the guy. No time like the present to find out. She pulled out her phone to call her. Luckily Zoey answered on the first ring.

"What's shakin' bacon?" Zoey said in a half whisper. "You are so not going to believe this, but I'm sitting out back, sipping my coffee, and all of a sudden I look off to my right, not a hundred and fifty feet from me, and see a moose. A moose! This place is amazing."

Izzy sighed. "Ugh. Don't be too jealous of me. I'm stuck

in traffic on the Santa Monica Freeway, bored out of my mind, and heard something on the radio about some guy in your town who's giving away a fancy engagement ring. What is up with that?" The traffic had slowed to a crawl, so Izzy quickly pulled an elastic off her wrist and caught her hair in a ponytail, then refocused her attention on the call on speakerphone. Well, and driving, of course, not that anyone was getting any driving done.

"Yeah, crazy, right?"

"You don't know him, do you?"

"Of course I do. In a town this size, you get to know pretty much everyone. Especially with Tanner's line of work."

"So what's the deal?" Izzy saw a gap in the left lane and manipulated her car into it as the driver laid on his horn and flipped her off. She reciprocated in kind. Damn, a girl could get a repetitive strain injury from flipping the finger while commuting in this town.

"He was engaged and she broke it off right before the wedding. It's been a year now and he's ready to get rid of the ring—it felt like a bad luck thing to keep it. Not like he'd ever use it again anyhow."

"Shit, I'd at least sell it. So he's *giving* it away? That seems crazy."

"Believe me, he doesn't need the money."

"Is he a nice guy?"

"He's great. Very chill. Laid back. Never heard a cross word out of his mouth."

"Great! I'm coming up to meet him." Izzy took the first exit she could and pulled over to program her Waze app to redirect her out of the traffic pileup.

"Okayyyy… That seems a bit extreme," Zoey said. "But I'd be happy to see you regardless. You know you're always welcome."

"Perfect. I'm going home to pack a bag and driving up there. I'll see you soon!"

Izzy always forgot what a long damned drive it was from LA to Bristol, a drive she'd done plenty of times since Zoey had transplanted herself there. It helped that it was right on the way to her place in Banff. But damn, she always felt like she'd been hit by a truck by the time she got there. It didn't help that instead of overnighting somewhere, she'd pull over and sleep every couple of hours. A quick peek in the mirror revealed that her usually lustrous, long, wavy dark hair looked like a fluffed-up dandelion on steroids. Her mascara, applied yesterday before she knew she was road tripping that very day, had raccooned beneath her eyes in a most attractive way to make her look like a maniacal Victorian-era slasher. Her unbrushed teeth felt as if they'd sprouted fur. She was sure she was a sight for only the sorest of eyes.

She wanted to grab a token hostess gift to bring to Zoey and Tanner and figured a bottle of wine would suffice. Parking her car on Main Street, she got out, walked the block or so to the wine shop, and marveled at the spectacular 360-degree mountain views set against a pristine blue sky. Even the air felt amazing here compared to the funk she breathed in regularly in LA, which sometimes seemed to come in chunks.

She was so busy staring at the scenery that she failed to pay attention to where she was walking, and before she knew it she'd stepped in a disgusting, fresh pile of doggy doo. Furious, she looked around to see who was responsible for it and up ahead saw a guy with a plaid shirt over a T-shirt and pair of shorts demanding that a nearby husky puppy with bright blue eyes come to him. The dog instead kept running circles around the sidewalk, defying his orders. He might as well have been flipping the finger at his owner, not to mention at Izzy and her mucked-up boots.

"You!" she said to the man, her voice rising higher the angrier she got thinking about it. All that crapola smeared over her nice cowboy boots, and now she had to get disgusting poop off of them before she could even get to Zoey and Tanner's.

The guy looked at her and pointed to himself, lifting a questioning brow.

"Yeah. You." She furrowed her forehead, then pointed at his pup. "Look what your damned dog did to me." She lifted her foot and showed him the smear on the sole of her boot that extended across the tip of the toe of the thing as well.

The guy stopped walking and stared at her, eyes opened wide.

"My dog?" He shook his head vigorously. "How do you know my dog did that?"

Izzy spread her arms out wide. "Um, do you see any other dog around?"

He frowned. "Not at this very minute, but that could have been left there hours ago by someone else's dog!"

"Not hardly," she said. "It's freshly laid if that's a term. Ugh. I cannot believe I'm parsing out terminology for dog poop." She growled. "Look, dude. Curb your damned dog. You owe me a pair of boots. I recently bought these things too." She wagged her finger at him as if that was going to achieve anything.

The guy approached her, his eyebrows knit, his lips

pursed. "Quit your bitching, lady. My dog didn't do that. But if it's going to make you happy, here." He grabbed his wallet from his back pocket and pulled a handful of bills from within, reaching for her hand and stuffing them into her palm. "Now you can go out and buy yourself a new pair. Go crazy with it."

With that, he turned away, whistled for his dog, and muttered loud enough for Izzy to hear, "Let's go, Blizzard, and get away from the crazy lady before she hurts you." He shook his head. "Fucking tourists."

Izzy looked down at the money in her hand and realized he'd jammed six one hundred dollar bills there. Six hundred freaking dollars. In her hand. To replace her boots. That she'd bought at TJ Maxx for about eighty bucks. Four years ago. Yeah, she knew she'd lied about them being new. But she'd wanted to make him feel extra bad.

Well, that certainly was a best-case scenario for her boots, even if the guy was a bit of a jerk. She didn't have time to replace the footwear right now, but with the cash in her hand, she removed the yucky one and dumped it in the trash can, limping the rest of the way back to her car, where she could put on another pair of shoes from her suitcase till she got to Zoey's. What an inauspicious beginning to her quest to meet the charming ring donor. The good news was at least he wouldn't be a complete asshole like that guy was.

Chapter Three

IF that didn't pluck his last nerve! That woman had some brass ones accusing him—and his sweet, innocent Blizzard—of dumping and running. Well, not that *he* would have done that, but his pup? Sure Blizzard had his moments of impropriety. He had a bad habit of sticking his nose in people's crotches, for instance, and he proudly showed off a damned yowl that sometimes set Sully's teeth on edge. But the poor pooch wasn't one to do what she'd so rudely accused him of.

At least he was able to shut her up with the cash. Not like he usually flaunted his wealth, but sometimes to simplify life you had to fix a problem—even one that wasn't self-created—with a few Ben Franklins.

"And then she had the nerve to blame me for it." He looked into the mirror to make eye contact with Carver Biscayne, proprietor of Snip It Good, the one and only barbershop in Bristol. If you couldn't confess your woes to a barber, who could you confess them to?

Carver, a sixty-something man who wore a cowboy hat even while cutting hair and sported an outdated handlebar moustache that extended across his face from ear to ear, shook his head. "Woman sounds uppity if you ask me." He had a hank of Sully's hair between his fingers and snipped with his scissors. "Was she pretty?"

Sully knit his brows. "What do her looks have to do with

her attitude?"

Carver continued clipping away. "Call me old-fashioned, but I think a pretty lady can get away with a lot more sassing back to strangers, is all."

Sully stuck out his lower lip as he mulled that over for a minute. Yes, she was quite attractive, but he hated having noticed. If he thought about it, her ice-blue eyes reminded him of Blizzard's baby blues. Although Blizzard's eyes were quite stunning, if anyone suggested she had dog eyes, he wasn't sure she'd like it. Those eyes were wasted on a boy. A boy dog at that.

She'd worn a cute little clingy sundress with spaghetti strings that exposed strong, tanned shoulders and a neckline that dipped so low he'd have had to be deaf, dumb, and blind not to notice her nice set of ta-tas. Not that he'd had long enough to stare, what with her machine-gunning her irrational accusations at him. But when she sashayed away, he sure as hell enjoyed seeing the swing of her hips with that cute little ass of hers taunting him so hypnotically.

Okay, so fine, she was pretty hot. But she was clearly the kind of woman you steered far away from. The last thing he needed was a pain-in-the-ass contrarian who would no doubt make his life miserable. He was happy as a pig in shit where he was despite the hottie with the boot in shit putting a damper on his day.

"So you gonna ask her out?"

Sully shook his head to be sure he was hearing properly. It made Carver's hand slip and the tip of his scissors took a tiny bite out of Sully's ear.

"Owww." He reached up to rub the wound only to see blood all over his fingertips when he pulled his hand away.

"Geez, Carver, maybe I should get you a butcher knife to finish the job."

Carver grinned. "I get my name honestly. Now answer the question."

"Question?"

Carver nodded. "Are you gonna ask her out?"

His customer puffed out a laugh of disbelief. "The day hell freezes, maybe?"

Carver held a slick slide of hair in his hands and looked up before cutting. "Sometimes those sassy ones are wild in bed." He chuckled. "Hot in the temper, hot in the sack."

Sully held his hands up. "In that case, I'll keep my eyes out for a boring, quiet librarian type. I've got no interest in a ballbuster as a prom date." He watched chunks of his hair fall to the ground as Carver's scissors danced. Hopefully he wouldn't end up with a buzz cut after all this.

"Besides, now that I think of it—that woman looked downright nuts. Her hair was sticking out all over the place." He pulled at the hair Carver wasn't cutting. "And the makeup smeared around her eyes made her look like a bloodthirsty zombie on a two-day bender. I'm glad I threw money at her to get her off my back. Tanner says Zoey's got some friend they want me to meet tonight, so at least I'll have some normal woman I can talk with instead of a cray-cray one." He pointed toward his head and circled his finger for emphasis.

Carver took out his poofy barber brush and dusted it across Sully's neck.

"Well, that is good news," he said. "You've been running off with those women for quickies for long enough. About time you meet a nice young thing you can show off around town."

Sully laughed. "Now I know you prefer your horse to your car, but I think you're putting the cart before the horse this time around. I haven't even met the woman, so let's not assume we're moving in together."

Carver gave him a friendly pat on the back. "I know, son. But I'm well aware of how hard it hit you when your girl left. We all want to see you happy again."

Sully's eyes opened wide. "Happy? Me—not happy?" He looked around and pointed out the window at the towering mountain range so close you could practically touch it. "I am downright ecstatic. I get to wake up here every morning. I can pretty much call the shots in my life. It would take a veritable act of God to make me not happy."

Carver gave him a thumbs-up. "That's what I like to hear, Sully. You're a man with a big heart and the voice of an angel. You should be happy."

He nodded, shaking out some loose pieces of hair. "And now that that woman is out of my hair, I'm all the better."

Chapter Four

AS soon as she got settled in, Izzy would have to buy new boots to replace the ruined pair. The nerve of that guy, ruining her go-to Montana footwear. After all, what self-respecting tourist would be caught dead in the state without a pair of sexy cowboy boots? She laughed at herself: it didn't matter that the cowboy boots on the locals were far from sexy, caked in mud and dung, and scratched all up and back. Although give her a man in cowboy boots and she'd show him what to do with those spurs. She had a fondness for the kind of guy who got his hands a little dirty, whose jeans were beat-up, who had a bit of sweat on his brow. So maybe the beat-up cowboy boots were sexier still, after all.

Well, for now she'd be happy to make it to Zoey's house, unpack her things, and clean up a bit.

She pulled down the long driveway, majestically lined with cottonwood trees. The air was so much fresher out here—the smell of pine filled the air. You could hear the wind whispering through the trees and the tall grass and see the wildflowers that had started to appear in the nearby fields.

Most of the time, she enjoyed living in LA. There was the ocean, of course. And so much to do: restaurants and museums and clubs, plus you could be in Mexico before you knew it or Hawaii or up to the wine country. But there were times when the idea of the solemnity of someplace like

Bristol, Montana had a certain appeal. Not that she'd ever end up here. Why would she? Her home was in LA as were her friends. Well, not her best friend—she was here now. And she could understand why. When Zoey met Tanner Eliasson, she was hit hard enough to chuck civilization for this altogether different lifestyle. Izzy wondered if she could make that break, but it was a moot point. There was nothing to draw her here—at least not enough to get her to change up her life for it. Even if her life of late had become kind of rote. Work was boring, and dating was annoying, especially in LA, where you had to be thin and young and, well, thin and young. If you weren't fifteen-and-a-half with at least one television pilot under your belt, you were washed up. It wasn't her scene so much anymore.

She parked her car in front of the sprawling log cabin-style home, grabbed her belongings, climbed the steps, and rang the doorbell.

"Iz! So glad you're here!" Zoey gave her friend a big hug and was thunked in the back by Izzy's boot, which she had been clutching in her hand. "Where'd you put your other boot?" Zoey reached for Izzy's suitcase and grabbed the bottle of wine her friend held out for her.

Izzy shook her head. "Honestly, I thought this was a nice town you lived in, full of friendly people. But I happened into some complete wanker of a guy on Main Street who encourages his dog to crap all over the sidewalk."

Zoey's eyebrows furrowed. "I'm sorry, but could you translate that into English for me please?"

Izzy shook out her hair, running her fingers through it to try to detangle it a bit.

Zoey held up her hand. "Dude, that's only making things worse. I'd recommend a good long shower and shampoo and you'll be much happier for it. In the meantime—the boot?"

"So I stopped in town to grab some wine—didn't want to come empty-handed especially after inviting myself. And as I was walking down the sidewalk, I stepped in *merde*, and then this guy and his dog were there and obviously it was his fault. And he was super rude and, well, my boot was all disgusting, and I knew it was never going to come clean, so I pitched it."

Zoey squinted at her. "But you kept one boot because?"

Her friend pursed her lips. "Wow. What a good question. I couldn't even begin to tell you. Blame it on the long drive. But the good news is these boots were actually kind of crap and he dumped a pile of money in my lap to replace them."

"So he was a polite rude person, then?"

"I wouldn't go that far. Let's say if I saw him again I would be more inclined to throw a drink in his face than to thank him for the new boots."

"Good thing you'll never see him again then." Zoey led Izzy through the warm, comfortable living room, down the hall to the guest bedroom.

"Oh, hurray, my surrogate kitty is here to greet me," Izzy said, scooping up Zoey's white Persian cat, Snowball. She smothered the cat with kisses all over her face. "Sometimes I think she's a dog, she's so tolerant of my affection."

"Well, listen, get yourself situated." Zoey pulled at her friend's hair, shaking her head. "And maybe shower and wash up. We'll pop into town for some boots and then meet up with Tanner at Harry's."

"And then I can meet Sully?"

Izzy nodded. "He's playing there tonight, so if he's not too busy, I'll make sure to introduce you to him."

"Sweet."

They took Zoey's car into town, diverting to the Boot Depot off Main Street. It didn't take Izzy long as they wandered through the store to find her dream shoe: a pair of distressed, brown, vintage leather boots that looked like they'd been lovingly shot to shit for years before being sold on the open market. Which they probably had. The top two inches of the boot sported pink, red, blue, and white embroidered wildflowers on them, with a garland of embroidered flowers bracketing along the ankle of the heeled boot as well. A leather zipper pull dangled from the zipper top as if letting the world know it had an important job to do. These were some kick-ass boots—you could dress them up or down, and they had to fit her feet like a glove.

Izzy held the boot up for her friend's approval.

Zoey held her thumbs up.

"Ooooee," she said as she dusted her hands together. "Those are the kind of boots you wouldn't even bother taking off before being taken by a hot cowboy."

Izzy cocked her head. "You mean that's a thing?"

Zoey shrugged. "Didn't you ever hear that line that country girls do it with their boots on?"

Izzy shook her head. "Guess I've not been living." She held the boot up and inspected it closely. "But now that you mention it, it would be kinda sexy to keep your boots on. Especially if he's got you up against a wall, beyond earshot of the dance hall." She closed her eyes to imagine that, then asked the sales clerk to bring a pair in her size. "God, I hope these fit now that I've got my plans in mind."

"Who, pray tell, are you planning to knock boots with?"

Her friend gave her shoulder a friendly shove. "Why the Prince of Bristol, of course!"

Zoey lifted an eyebrow. "Prince of Bristol?"

"The ring guy, silly!"

Zoey crooked her finger and motioned for Izzy to come closer.

"I hate to break it to you, sweetie, but I'm afraid Sully's not exactly dating material."

"Oh, he will be. He's not met me yet."

"While I admire your degree of self-confidence, it's not that simple. As long as I've been here, Sully's been a no-woman man. And by that I mean he's never even seen with a woman except slipping away from a bar with an anonymous tourist, then maybe slipping away from her hotel room in the middle of the night afterward."

"So, he's a player?"

Zoey pursed her lips in thought. "I'm not sure if he's a player, per se. It's more like after his fiancée ditched him, he was pretty bitter. The last thing on his mind was a relationship with a woman. I think he basically worked his way through every eligible woman on holiday here for a good year."

"Ewww. Let's hope he wore a condom."

Zoey rolled her eyes. "For any number of reasons. But, yeah, I don't think he's the kind of guy who deliberately uses a woman, necessarily, but I think he's gun-shy. He was pretty devastated when Gretchen bailed on him—he took it personally."

Izzy rolled her eyes. "In his defense, how could you not? I mean it's not like he got turned down for a job he was interviewing for. He'd already done the legwork, they'd made the wedding plans, it was all systems go, and she chickened out? I'd take that personally too!"

"My point is I don't think you should be scurrying down to the courthouse for your wedding license or anything. Even if Sully thinks you're the greatest thing to hit the plains since the buffalo, I can pretty much assure you he's going to need a lot of time before he is on board with trusting a woman and allowing himself to be part of a couple. Consider yourself warned."

"To think I drove all the way here to marry him." She gave her friend a wink and paid cash for her boots.

Chapter Five

SULLY mounted the four flights of steps to get to Harry's rooftop, guitar and Blizzard in tow. Blizzard had started this rather annoying habit of yowling like a woman in the throes of labor, and he hoped he didn't choose to show off his doleful cry while he was playing tonight. You could say it was a cute thing, but it was annoying as hell.

He hated to draw attention to himself and having your dog make a scene would definitely do that. Hell, even today, that woman made a damned scene about the dog, but it was directed at Sully, big-time, and he hated that. Especially since he was innocent on all charges. That sort of thing lingered with him, and he kept alternating between feeling embarrassed and being ticked at that woman for accusing him.

But he needed to clear his head and get ready to perform. What happened earlier today was over and done with, and dwelling on it wasn't going to help him put on a good show. He walked out onto the rooftop bar and was greeted by a throng of people. He stood there, feet planted, eyes darting left and right, first off wondering how he was going to make his way through the crowd with his guitar (not to mention his pup), and second, what the hell? It was a Wednesday night for God's sake. Granted the season was picking up and with it the crowds. But this was like nothing he'd experienced since he'd started playing here. He even saw a couple of reporters interspersed in the crowd. Weird.

He angled himself sideways and started shouldering his way through the mass of people. Out of nowhere, things got bizarrely quiet, and the crowd parted ways for him. Someone squealed, and a woman with a high-pitched voice shouted out, "There he is!" and the next thing he knew all of these women were shouting out his name. His eyes grew wide. Wondering what the fuck was going on, he continued to press toward the front of the bar area where he knew a stool and a mic awaited him. There he could regroup and try to figure out what was the deal.

Except that women were reaching for him—like touching him as if he were Michael Jackson, or maybe Jesus—hollering his name and trying to get a piece of him. At long last, he saw Angie, the bar manager, who reached out a hand and pulled him toward the front.

His eyes still wide open in stupefaction, he kept shaking his head.

"What—"

"Well, well, well, Mr. Magnanimous," Angie said with a broad grin. "Bet you didn't expect this." She spread her arms out wide.

"Mr. Magnanimous?" He scrunched his brows, his back deliberately turned to the crowd as he reached his stool.

She nodded. "Um, rumor has it you're holding some sort of contest to give away an engagement ring?"

When he opened his mouth to speak, nothing came out. Reaching for Blizzard, he squatted down to give him a hug.

"What hell hath you unleashed?" She elbowed him in the ribs as he stood up.

He shook his head. "Ch-rist. Goes to show no good deed goes unpunished. Please, Angie, I beg of you: save me from these women. And the reporters. The whole thing."

She pulled him back behind the far end of the bar to keep women from pushing in toward him. "So was this an impulse thing?"

He stared, absentmindedly shaking his head. "I sure as hell didn't plan on this." He heaved a sigh. "I wanted to do something nice."

"And now you've got a fan club that wants to express their unrequited gratitude for your munificence."

He cocked a brow at Angie, who had the weathered face of a woman who'd lived a hard life. In her defense, maybe it was the face of a woman who'd spent her whole life outside and the sun had beaten her to shit. And her brittle gray hair, braided in a ponytail that reached her butt, added to that narrative in his head. But she hadn't ever struck him as the kind of woman to use a word like that.

"Munificence? Now we're using ten-dollar words? I might have to open up my dictionary app to see what that even means."

She glared at him. "What would you like me to say, smart-ass?"

He grinned. "Stupidity, maybe?"

She laughed. "Yeah, that seems to go without saying. So why did you decide to do something so public?"

He shrugged. "Hell, I didn't think of it as public as much as casting a broad net. I wanted to be inclusive. Not launch a casting call for 'who wants to date the schmuck who didn't realize giving away an engagement ring would put a fucking bull's-eye on his head.'"

Angie reached into the cooler and grabbed a can of Sully's go-to beers, a Going to the Sun IPA.

"You want it in a frosted glass?"

He cocked his head toward her and smirked. "Me? You know I'm not one for pretenses, Ang. But I might need a

30

second one in about five minutes." He grabbed the beer and took a long, hard swig. "If I'm going to have to face this crowd like I'm some sort of teen heartthrob for all of these supposedly swooning women, I'm definitely gonna need more than one of these."

Angie let out a long, fake sigh. "You're like Bristol's very own Justin Bieber!"

"Thanks. Minus the bad boy behavior."

"There's still time." She winked at him.

"Is there still time to maybe reverse the clock and change my mind about the manner in which I plan to unload this stupid albatross of a ring?"

She put her arm over his shoulder. "Ahhh… You think of it as a ring, but it's so much more than that."

"Do tell."

"See, at first it was a symbol of betrothal. Of your love and commitment to the woman you chose to spend the rest of your life with."

"So it's a sign of stupidity."

She held up a finger. "No. Now, hear me out."

He shook his head. "Fine. But you'd better be fast. I'm supposed to start in a few minutes."

"I'll make this quick. So when what's-her-name did what she did—"

"She-who-shall-not-be-named."

Angie nodded. "Yes, her. So, her leaving you meant that the ring then morphed into so much more. A symbol of betrayal, of loss, of hurt. It went from being a thing of such beauty to a thing of contempt."

He nodded. "You're not telling me anything I don't already know. This is why I'm trying to unload it. Although I should've chucked it into the river to be done with it."

"But this is where the symbolism gets even better.

31

Because you didn't do that. See, you're a man of great wealth. Throwing that ring into the river would have been easy for you to do. You didn't need that money back, whereas for most people, that represents a large chunk of change that they spend years saving for. Either that or going into hock for."

He nodded. "I know, I know. I can't help it I didn't have to suffer financially for it."

"I'm not blaming you—I'm explaining why these women"—she pointed out to the shoulder-to-shoulder packed crowd—"all went out of their way to come here. It's because of you. You, who could've trashed the ring, decided to return the ring to its original emotional luster as it were. You are, to all of these women—not to mention, I'd presume, to a crapton of women across the world right now—a good guy. Like it or not, you now represent the best of your gender." She ran her fingers through his hair. "Fact is, if I were twenty years younger, I'd be out there swooning for you too."

His eyes grew large again. "That's quite a burden to carry. I'm not the saint they think I am."

"Maybe not a saint, but you're likely a far cry better than the guys they're used to. And that means a lot to a lot of women." She swatted his butt affectionately. "Now get out there and give those ladies what they want."

He laughed. "I'm afraid I don't have enough sexual stamina to give them what *they* want."

She winced. "I'm afraid your days of slipping off with the tourist du jour are gone for now too."

He nodded slowly, the reality of that dawning on him. "Well, crap. There is that. Although to be honest it was starting to feel a little hollow."

"Maybe that's a sign it's time to put yourself out there

again."

"In a sea of this?" He nodded toward the crowd. "I might have to join a monastery if this doesn't go away soon."

"Somehow, I suspect a lifetime of celibacy isn't in the cards for you."

It was his turn to wince. "Good Lord, no. I'm going to have to find a regular booty call, some woman not looking for commitment but only a means to an end."

"Like you said, might be time for a monastery. Now go sing about heartbreak and unrequited love and make those ladies cry."

"Will you give me an armed escort out of here later on?"

She flexed her guns. "How about a well-armed bartender manager. I can fend off aggressive women for you. I earned these biceps with years of chopping firewood, clearing brush, working my farm."

"You're looking more like my kinda gal by the minute, Ang." He leaned over and kissed the top of her head.

Chapter Six

"HOLY cannoli." Izzy had trudged up four flights of steps, trying to keep up with Zoey, who was evidently in much better shape now that she was working on Tanner's ranch instead of killing herself at Soul Cycle in West Hollywood. *Note to self… maybe you get even more fit living an outdoor life in the middle of nowhere.* When they got to the top of the steps, they were confronted with a crowd of primarily women who blocked the way to even get to the bar.

Izzy scrunched her brows. "I had no idea this town was so popular. I mean it's a Wednesday night for goodness' sakes."

"Wait a sec—Tanner sent me a text." Zoey held up her phone and read it, then nodded. "Oh my God. This—" She extended her arms. "This is all because of that ring thing."

Realization dawned on Izzy. Of course. She wouldn't be the only woman charmed by the altruistic gesture of a scorned man. Well, crap. There goes any chance of meeting Mr. Perfect.

"Sooo… Guess this means me and Ring Man aren't going to—" She crossed her fingers in a sign of intimacy.

Zoey shook her head. "Sweetie, Izzy. You didn't honestly think you were going to drive up here and have sex with the man and everything would be great, did you?"

Izzy frowned. "Well, no. But there is this fantasy version of reality that would make the whole meet-cute-slash-end-up-together thing happen, you know? I mean it happens in movies all the time."

Zoey shook her head. "You've been living in Los Angeles for too long."

"Seriously. I did not expect I'd go in for the kill with the man the minute I met him. But I had imagined that since you guys were friends, we'd sit here and enjoy listening to him play, and when he was done, we'd all have drinks together and laugh and I'd charm him with my witty banter and he'd invite me out on a date for tomorrow and we'd have so much fun at dinner he'd invite me back to his place where we would decidedly not sleep together. I mean nothing wrong with that, but I don't want to blow this by being too forward, you know? But maybe we'd make out, like a lot, and maybe get a little handsy, but in a good way, and we'd have another date or two and sure, eventually we'd hook up—but not in a hookup way but in a romantic way—and next thing you know we'd be dating exclusively and who knows where that would lead."

Zoey stood there, staring at her friend, eyes wide open.

"You're in need of a good man in your life, aren't you?"

Izzy frowned. "I don't know, Zoey. I'm kind of lonely. And tired of loser-type guys who aren't date material, let alone boyfriend material."

"I understand, I do," her friend said. "But let's set aside your rom-com fantasies about this and can you just be you—the normal, sweet, fun, vivacious, and kind-of-weird you and not this desperate-seeming harpy who wants to win the prize?"

"Harpy? I think I'm insulted."

"You know what I mean. I don't mean harpy in a bad way. I mean turn off the aggressive 'must have man now' thing and be Izzy. If and when you meet, let things transpire organically. Don't try to force it."

Izzy heaved a sigh. "Okay, I know it. You're so right about this. I have totally lost perspective. We might be completely incompatible and here I am being all 'he's my perfect dream guy.' He might even have bad breath. Or creepy sexual fetishes. Maybe he's one of those guys who shaves his legs—I totally couldn't do that. I dated a cyclist once and I'm sorry, but I like hair on a guy's legs."

Zoey palmed her friend's face. "You are so weird. Look, let's try to work our way somewhere within listening distance so we can hear his music and then figure out meeting up with Sully when we can, 'kay? Tanner's saving us seats but it might be a while till we can get anywhere near them because he's up front. In the meantime, our best move is to try to get to the bar. At least then we can drink."

"A few well-placed elbows would help us to get to where we need to be."

"Yeah, but that would be part of the man-killer mentality you're trying to avoid, remember?"

"Right. I forgot for a minute."

"Oh, but, look." She pointed toward the mountains, with the late-day sun painting them in a wash of melon hues. "This is one of the reasons I love it here so much."

Izzy took in the skyline—a far different skyline from what she was used to back home. And admittedly it had far more appeal and much less smog.

"At first, I wondered about you moving here," she said. "But I am starting to get it. This place isn't LA, for sure, but it's got a whole lot that LA can't even compete with."

"Like a moose while you're drinking coffee."

"Yeah, that. And I'm telling you I'd better see a mother bear and her babies while I'm here or I'll feel robbed."

Zoey nodded. "It is something to behold. From a safe

distance, that is."

"Dude. I can handle the men of LA. I think I can take on a baby grizzly."

The two laughed as they reached the edge of the bar. Zoey caught the eye of someone behind the bar.

"Angie—what a sight for sore eyes! Any chance you can grab us a couple of beers? My friend Izzy just got into town and needs to decompress from her type A existence."

Angie grinned.

"I've got a feeling half the women here are doing the same thing. While they wait for their Prince Charming to take a break so they can charm him with their feminine wiles."

Izzy decided to keep her mouth shut about her original intent for this road trip. It had been foolish at best to think this was a good idea. Instead she would relax and enjoy her time in Bristol, listen to some good music, and hopefully see a family of grizzlies before she returned to the dating rat race back home.

Just then she heard the singer—Sully, what was his last name? Forester? Yes, Sully Forester—whose haunting voice was so darned smooth and soft and gentle and sexy. It was the kind of voice that seduced you, made love to you, like John Mayer's, a little playful, very seductive. Wow. If she was not going to be smitten by him, she could at least be smitten by his voice. She closed her eyes and took in the song about a love that didn't last, about the pain of losing but the hope of getting over it. Hopeful. That's what she heard in his voice: a sense of buoyant optimism in the face of heartache. She loved the encouragement behind his words. It felt like a message she needed to listen to. So what that she came here for a superficial purpose. Now that she was here, she'd absorb the surroundings, enjoy time with her girl, and not worry about forcing her bizarre temporary insanity plan into action.

She'd meet the guy sooner or later, no big deal. Even if they didn't hit it off on that level, she was sure they'd have a perfectly fine time hanging with Zoey and Tanner for the evening if that's what happened. It was all good.

Chapter Seven

SULLY was not one to enjoy crowds. They made him antsy, especially on the roof of a building and tempted him to climb over the edge and take a flying leap. The only salvation was that up here in front of the hordes of mostly women, there was an invisible no-go line and he could hold them at bay. He was deathly afraid that the minute he decided to take a break, they would violate that unspoken space delineator and go in for the kill. God, he needed another beer.

Out of the corner of his eye, he caught Tanner off to the side, covetously guarding two other chairs, despite the steady stream of strangers who kept trying to filch them. The upside of being a local meant you didn't care who wanted your seat; if you were saving it for your significant other, it was, for all intents and purposes, reserved. Yet he wondered who the third was for. Those two were usually together thick as thieves on their own. In between songs, he had the brilliant idea to text Tanner to save him from the mob. In most cases, Sully would have been fine if one woman was after him. He'd gladly take advantage of the moment as long as the feeling was mutual. But all those women were sort of scaring him.

He shot Tanner a text and received a response as he started strumming a few bars on his guitar, getting ready for his last song before it was time for a break. He swigged from his nearby water bottle and casually glanced at his phone to see what Tanner wrote.

Dude, I got your back. Come over here as soon as you finish the song. I'll give you a seat and Zoey can sit on my lap. A win-win. She has someone she wants you to meet anyhow.

Huh. Here's hoping it wasn't yet another one of these women out for a scrap of his flesh.

He finished his song then set down his guitar and turned off his mic, standing up to make his way to Tanner's seat. But a damned reporter nabbed him first.

The woman wedged her microphone right up into his face as her cameraman veered a little, backing into people and almost tripping over Blizzard in the process to try to get the shot.

"Hey, Sully—Brittney Beasley from News Nine. A few minutes of your time?"

She didn't wait to let him answer that. If it was a question or a statement, he wasn't sure. Instead she pushed the mic closer to his mouth.

"So, what do you think about the reaction to the ring auction?"

He squinted, pulling a bandana from his back pocket to wipe some sweat from his brow.

"It's not an auction."

She waved her hands dismissively. "Freebie, giveaway, whatever."

"Yeah, well, I'm simply looking for someone who might want it."

She laughed. "Pretty sure everyone here does, for starters." She spread her free arm out. "Though I have a feeling they want you with it."

He rolled his eyes. "Yeah, well."

"What do you think of that?"

He shook his head. "I'm sorry. I've got somewhere to be."

"Is there a new lady in your life? Is that what precipitated this?"

He waved away the microphone with his hand and started walking toward Tanner.

He gave a quick whistle for his pup though figured he couldn't hear it over the din anyhow.

As he hurried toward Tanner's seats, trying to avoid eye contact with everyone in the place, he couldn't help but glance up, only to see the last woman on the planet he wanted to see tonight throwing him a dirty look that would curl your hair.

As if this night wasn't bad enough, it was now substantially worse. He scrambled over to Tanner and plunked himself down, pulling Blizzard close for the false sense of protection he lent. Boy did he need another beer.

"What the hell is that jerk doing sitting with Tanner?" Izzy hissed out a bit louder than she thought. Everyone nearby turned and stared. Izzy and Zoey been far enough away from the singer that they could only hear him, not see him, during his set. It wasn't till he took a break that they were able to maneuver through the crowds toward the seats Tanner had been saving. But with that guy there, Izzy wanted nothing to do with going over there.

"What jerk?"

"That's the guy. The mean guy I met today. The one who ruined my boot."

Zoey turned toward Izzy and stood still.

"Ummm… You do realize who that is, don't you?"

"Of course I do. I mean I don't know the guy's name, but believe me, I never forget a face. Especially one that belongs to the likes of him."

Zoey started to laugh as she playfully slapped her friend on the shoulder. "Sweetie. You are badmouthing just about the kindest man within two hundred miles of this bar."

"What are you talking about?" Izzy could barely disguise her annoyance, deliberately throwing daggers his way for good measure.

Zoey pointed at Sully, then pointed at her left ring finger, then nodded.

"I still have no idea what you're saying."

"Izzy, honey. That's Sullivan Forester."

Her jaw slackened and she was without words for a minute.

"By Sullivan do you mean Sully?"

Her friend nodded. "One and the same."

"Well, crap. You've fixed me up with the guy who doesn't curb his dog?"

Zoey did a double take, then twisted her finger in her ear as if trying to clear it of something so she could hear better.

"Wait a second. *Me?* fixing *you* up?"

Izzy frowned. "Well…"

"Well, I seem to recall that a certain someone heard about the magnanimous Mr. Forester's lovely gesture and called and begged me to fix her up with him. Ring any bells?"

Heat raced up Izzy's face. "You're making me feel foolish, you know."

"Iz, we're best friends, right? So I'm gonna put it out there because best friends don't lie to one another."

"Okaaay…"

"You're being foolish, which is why you feel foolish. Don't get me wrong, I welcomed the idea of your visit—any occasion is fine by me! But it did seem a little daft to race up here for some fantasy you hoped would come to life."

Izzy held her hands up. "I know! I'm with you. But I'd already acknowledged to myself that I was here for the wrong reasons. Now it's not only am I here for the wrong reasons and already decided I didn't want to force myself on this Sully guy, but now, crap, he's the jerky guy. That's like a double whammy."

"So let's try a little practice in mindfulness, okay? We're going to go over there and I'm going to introduce you and you are going to behave like the normal woman I know and love, not the insane stalker you somehow morphed into over the past few days. And even if you think Sully's dog did his business on the sidewalk, I feel strongly you're wrong about that—Sully's not that kind of guy—but also maybe you should let it go. It's over and done with. You got a new pair of gorgeous boots, and you're here enjoying a beer and the great outdoors and maybe we'll go hiking and search for grizzly babies before you go back home. Deal?"

"I'd rather behave like a grizzly mama, to be honest."

"Izzy…"

"You know you told me he was a nice guy and never said bad words."

"He is nice."

"He swore at me! Called me a fucking tourist. And he doesn't curb his damned dog."

"Blizzard is not a 'damned dog.' He is cute and adorable and precious. Now be a good girl and don't make a scene."

"Puh-lease. I couldn't even if I wanted to. Look at him, women pawing all over him. I'd sooner have voluntary surgery than spend time with him."

"Well, then fake it because we're going over there in three, two, one."

Chapter Eight

SULLY tried to remind himself that he had landed in a pubescent boy's wet dream. Women were as close to hanging on to him as they could be without actually doing so. One woman had come up and combed her fingers through his hair, then dragged her nails along his scalp till the hairs on his neck stood up. Who knew head-scratching was an erogenous stimulant? He feared he'd have to tame down his dick if this didn't stop, pronto. He sure as hell couldn't go back up there in front of the mob with a bulge in his pants. Then again, it would probably please this crowd.

So far, two women had already slipped him their hotel keys. Another leaned over and whispered that she had mad skills going down on men. Which begged the question, how many times did it take practicing that skill to refine such a talent?

Perhaps he was getting too old for this. Or maybe he merely thought he was. After all, what self-respecting man would complain about a woman offering herself up, no strings attached? Wasn't that what he'd been doing for the past year? Mutually agreed-upon booty calls, no strings, no nothing but temporary fun in the moment. Yet hookups had already started to feel so empty, and now came this crazy, unexpected, and seriously overwhelming situation.

He kept eyeing his watch, getting his head around going

back to performing as a way to escape the madness that had befallen this place. But then the madness got even weirder.

"Hey, Tanner, Sully." Sully looked up to see Tanner's girlfriend Zoey, her hand secured around the wrist of none other than that woman from earlier in the day. The accuser. It looked like Zoey was practically dragging her toward them. As if on cue, Blizzard got up and jumped up against the mean woman, leaving damp spots from her paws (which had been planted in spilled beer) on her dress.

Tanner intervened and pulled Blizzard away before he caused more problems.

Awkward moment number 264 for the evening.

"So, uh, Sully, this is my very best friend in the whole wide world, Isabelle Strong. We call her Izzy. I told her she would just love you, by the way." She gave an exaggerated wink. It was clear she was trying to do damage control for her friend.

He looked over to see Izzy rolling her eyes.

"Huh," he said as he stood up and crossed his arms. He took a few tight steps around her, then scratched his chin, which was sporting a couple of days of beard growth. "Interesting that you got that so wrong, Zoey. Because I'd say it's more like she loves to hate me."

Izzy glared.

"I think Izzy was about to apologize to you for that little misunderstanding this afternoon. Weren't you, Iz? Did I mention she's my very best friend?" Zoey tugged on her friend's arm and pushed her toward Sully so the two were only inches away from each other, both with their arms crossed, lips pursed. It was like a showdown. The tension was finally broken by the sudden and unexpected mournful wails of Blizzard, who'd jumped up in between them and proceeded to yowl like a cat in heat, loud enough that it seemed the entire bar turned to see what was going on.

Izzy was the first to burst out laughing.

"It sounds like that dog of yours is in the throes of some seriously heady sex."

Sully stood back and fixed his gaze on her. Why did the mere mention of sex near this annoying woman trigger something in him? It couldn't be her fiery temper. He was never one to go for a woman who went from zero to sixty in an instant. Then again, maybe there was something to that. What was the saying—hot in the head, hot in the bed? Or did he make that one up? Here he had all these gorgeous women fawning all over him tonight and he'd found them all thoroughly uninteresting. Yet a fleeting handful of minutes with this little diva friend of Zoey's and his curiosity was already piqued.

"If that's the most arousing sounds you've heard while having sex, you might not have been having it with the right men." Sully took a swig from his beer.

Izzy uncrossed her arms.

"Well, no shit, Sherlock," she said. "That's precisely why I'd originally come up here to meet you."

Sully started choking on his beer, which had apparently gone down the wrong pipe.

"I beg your pardon?"

"I'd heard about your thing and I was intrigued. It's no secret in my world that I've been dating losers exclusively. Ask Zoey." She pointed to her friend, who nodded and shrugged. "I figured you sounded like a dream come true. So thoughtful and sweet and considerate. But then I get up here and—"

Zoey held up her hand. "Izzy…"

Izzy cleared her throat, crossed her ankles, and stuck her hands in her pockets, hanging her head low. "Sorry." She then muttered something that Sully could've sworn was "sorry, not sorry," but it was fleeting and the place was so loud, it was hard to discern anything spoken sotto voce.

"Sorry for?" He couldn't help himself; he *had* to stick it to her.

She clenched her teeth hard and made one of those grrrr sounds. "For possibly wrongfully flipping out on you for something that wasn't your fault." She bit her lip and he wanted so damned badly to bite it for her it was killing him.

The corner of his mouth turned up into a grin. Making her suffer was kind of fun.

"So, you mean I gave you all that money to replace your boots for nothing?"

Zoey lifted a brow. "He paid for them, Iz?"

Izzy blushed. "Well, technically I paid for them. In that I handed the cashier the money for them."

Sully held up his hands. "It's not a big deal, Zoey. Really, don't sweat it."

"It is a big deal," Izzy said. "If I'm going to give you the benefit of the doubt and presume your dog—and you—were innocent, then I shouldn't allow the charade of your rightfully replacing my boots to continue. Let me make it up to you somehow."

Hoo boy, he could think of some deserving paybacks, though they would be entirely inappropriate under the circumstances. Shame, that.

He scratched his chin again, thinking hard of some way to exact not revenge but something a little less malicious. Penance, maybe?

"So I've got a little job to do tomorrow... I promised Mrs. Mullaney that I'd help repair some of her fencing."

Tanner leaned in. "Eleanor's husband died six months after a brief illness, and she's living on a large ranch they owned together. She has an occasional farmhand helping with the horses, but without Jed around, a lot of chores are going undone."

"Sooo… you're suggesting that I, a city girl, go along with you to help mend fences? On a ranch? When I've never stepped foot on a ranch, let alone know what a fence on a ranch looks like?"

Sully cocked his brow her way and shrugged. "Well, if the boot fits, wear it."

Izzy looked at Zoey and shook her head. "Why do I get the feeling I've been played?"

Her friend patted her on the head. "It'll be okay, Iz. Besides, you wanted to get alone time with the ring man, right? Now's your chance."

Izzy flipped her friend the finger as she turned on her heel.

Zoey quirked a brow. "I guess we'll be leaving now." She leaned over and kissed Tanner. "See you at home, babe." With a nod at Sully, she gave him a thumbs-up, the universal sign for "good job." Or "up yours," depending on which culture you're in, which could have been fitting under the circumstances. "Good luck with that one."

He started to laugh. "Ohhh, I think this could be quite amusing. Thanks for the challenge."

She gave him a wink. "I aim to please."

"Nice boots, by the way," Sully shouted at Izzy as she walked away.

Izzy turned and mimicked her friend with a pronounced thumbs-up, in the universal symbol for "okay." Only in this case, Sully was pretty certain she meant "up yours." And for some reason, he was good with that. He rather enjoyed having this feisty woman shoveling a mountain of shit on him—as long as that remained figurative not literal. With her, you might never know what she was capable of.

Chapter Nine

"'NICE boots,' he says to me. Nice freaking boots." Izzy was practically growling as she pulled her new-old boots on, preparing for her day from hell.

"I think it was a compliment," Zoey said, taking a sip of coffee as she stood by her grumbling friend.

"Compliment my ass," she said. "It was a final dig meant to get me riled up."

"Well, it seems it worked."

"Even worse. Why is it every time I hear him saying that in my head it makes me horny? Like my whole fantasy about doing it with your boots on up against a wall is running on an endless loop in my head."

"Wait—so you *do* still want to knock boots with him?"

Izzy glared at her. "Are you kidding me? You would not catch me dead with my skirt hiked up and my boots locked around his ass."

Zoey laughed. "For being so vehemently opposed to the idea, you sure have painted quite a vivid image."

Izzy sighed as she stood up. "Yeah, well, I'm in a dry spell, so all I've got is fantasies."

Zoey swatted her on the butt. "In that case, go forth and work on making those fantasies a reality, lady."

Izzy threw her a "yeah right" kind of look. "Uh, no. Not gonna happen. I've got my pride."

"What's that they say about pride cometh before a fall?"

"Maybe it's pride falleth before a come?"

"On that note, good luck being a cowgirl today. I'll be thinking of you!"

Twenty minutes later, Izzy had entered the Lazy L & R Ranch and was stepping onto the wraparound porch at the home of the widow Mullaney. Who she expected to be about ninety years old, but it turns out she was more like seventy and rather beautiful with striking white hair cut in a bob and bright blue eyes that twinkled when she smiled. She sported a denim button-down over a white T-shirt, a beat-up pair of jeans, and the ubiquitous boots that it seemed everyone wore around here. She looked as though she was about to go take on the chore Izzy was here to undertake.

Unfortunately Izzy had arrived early—curse her punctuality—before her nemesis, so she was going have to make small talk with the woman under rather awkward circumstances.

"Lovely to see you," Eleanor—she insisted Izzy call her by her first name—said. "So, are you the one who's sweet on our Sully? Can't say that I blame you. If I were twenty years younger, I'd be sinking my claws into him myself." She winked at her.

There was someone sweet on that man? That was news to her. Well, not so much. Women were glomming on him like white on rice at the bar last night. Clearly it was an unoriginal idea to seek out the Benevolent Mr. Forester to bask in his magnanimity. Whatever that meant. So yeah, even if she was still hot on the idea of him, she had seriously soured on the reality of the man, and it was probably a blessing in disguise. It would be awful to be head over heels for a guy who was the most sought-after man in all the country right now. Even the reporters there last night were making googly eyes at Sully.

After she'd made her dramatic exit last night, she realized she was still stuck at Harry's since she'd ridden in with Zoey, who was not ready to leave yet because she wanted to sit with Tanner to enjoy listening to Sully play.

So Izzy stayed back and observed from a distance. She saw at least two female reporters worm their way into interviews with Sully who looked disinterested at best, uncomfortable at worst. At least he came across as humble and not a cocky jerk. After that unpleasant episode earlier in the day, she found it a struggle to stop assigning him that unkind attribute. She made a note to try to be less judgy with the guy. Easier said than done. For some reason, something about him got under her skin. And perhaps in her psyche a bit.

"Can I get you an iced tea? I think it's going to be hot today—you'll need to stay hydrated." She lifted the pitcher on the table in front of her and poured two glasses. Izzy took a long, slow sip, which cooled her throat going down and felt so refreshing even before she'd lifted a finger to do work. "So how long have you two been dating?"

Izzy spat out the tea, making quick work to pretend she was stupidly choking on the drink, not the words. After wiping the tea from her mouth and shirt, she held up her hands.

"Oh no, I'm afraid you've got that wrong." She shook her head. "We only just met. I'm here helping out as, well, kind of a favor. Like a payback favor."

Eleanor frowned. "I feel bad that you're working for me

to pay him back."

"No worries. I'm happy to help out. It was kind of, well, I guess a huge misunderstanding, but it means I did something stupid and, ugh, never mind. Suffice it to say, he and I are virtual strangers."

The sound of boots on the porch steps prompted her to turn and see Sully approaching. He still hadn't shaved that scruff and it looked so freaking sexy, she wanted to run her hands along it. Wait—where did that stupid notion come from?

"Hi, babe, sorry I'm late," Sully said as he came up and out of nowhere, hugged her tight, and planted his lips on hers. Time came to a complete standstill as Izzy realized that a) his lips were on hers, b) his lips felt amazing on hers, c) he had the audacity to slip his tongue between her willing, betraying lips and before she knew it their tongues were dueling as well as their personalities seemed to, and d) she wanted nothing more than to stay here doing this for, oh, ever.

My God, the man could kiss. Her pulse quickened, her chest kind of heaving into his as her breathing became heavy. He had her pulled so close to him if she didn't do something immediately, she was going to end up with her back against the wall of Eleanor Mullaney's cedar shake siding with her skirt hiked up above her hips and her boots locked at the ankles around Sully's firm, just-the-right-size ass, which her hands were mysteriously grasping at right now. Right when she thought she'd shamelessly go to plan B up against the wall, Sully unceremoniously broke away.

"Oh, Eleanor, I'm so sorry. That was terribly rude of me. But I needed to say hello to my friend Izzy who I was so excited to see." He made air quotes when he said the word "friend." What the hell was he playing at?

She squinted at him.

"Sully, so great to see you." Eleanor got up and hugged him. "I don't expect I'll get quite the same greeting as Miss Izzy here. Who was telling me you two are virtual strangers." She gave him a wink.

He nodded. "Yeah, well, it's early days, Eleanor, and Izzy wants to keep her cards close to her chest. You know how these things go."

Izzy attempted to set the record straight but was met with resistance. "You've got it all wrong," she said. "It's only about this pair of boots I have to pay him back for—"

"Are those not the sexiest boots you've ever seen, Eleanor?" Sully said as he licked his lips. He licked his freaking lips. God help her she was not going to get through this day in an innocent fashion if he kept doing things like that.

Chapter Ten

SULLY wasn't quite sure how it was that he randomly went for the jugular with Isabelle Strong but damn, was he grateful he'd had the gumption to do it. Because wow, when his lips settled on hers, and she let him slip his tongue inside her mouth, there were fireworks behind his eyelids and his pulse sped up to NASCAR level. Maybe it was the way her jeans fit so snugly and emphasized that squeezable booty he'd eyed when she walked away from him. Or maybe it was those sexy boots that were emblematic of what got him so juiced up to begin with. Who knows? What he'd experienced during that kiss was so beyond his expectations, it was as if he'd tasted the best dessert on the menu and wanted to dine on it regularly.

He'd been halfway prepared for her to slap him for being so forward, but instead he was pleasantly surprised that she pretty much immediately yielded to his quite uncharacteristic impulses. Sure, he'd been happily going home with a host of willing women this past year, but it wasn't like him to up and mash his face to a woman who'd expressed overt annoyance with him.

Maybe deep down he wanted to prove to her he wasn't the bad guy. Because he wasn't the bad guy! He was a dude trying to make his way in the world, minding his business. Albeit now all of a sudden being treated like some bizarre hero, which he most decidedly wasn't. For crying out loud, all he wanted was to give the damned ring away.

Right now, he needed to get Izzy away from Eleanor so that things didn't turn sour. And maybe he could try to get to know her while she seemed quasi-receptive. He reached for her hand and linked fingers with hers. She looked at him like he'd sprouted a horn from his forehead.

"We'd better get to work—we've got hours ahead of us," he said. "Let's go out in my truck. I've got all the tools we'll need in the bed."

Yep, he had all the tools he'd need in any sort of bed with this one. As long as she didn't keep a pair of loppers handy for when she decided to get explosive.

He helped her into the cab where she got to sit next to Blizzard, who lavished her with kisses while Sully waved off Eleanor.

"You two lovebirds have fun!" she said, holding her hand up and waving with her fingers.

He hopped into the driver's seat and shut the door, pulling away and hoping for no repercussions. He learned quickly that he was living in a fantasy world if he expected none.

She turned toward him. "What the hell was that?"

He squinted, running his tongue along his teeth as he pondered the right response.

"What?"

"That!" She shoved her arm toward the house in dramatic fashion like she was thrusting a fencing épée into her opponent. And it was sort of a lunge with a verbal sword.

"You mean when she called us lovebirds?" He grinned.

"I mean that and when you wove your fingers with mine as if we were a piece of damned tapestry. And when you jammed your tongue down my throat like you were fishing for my breakfast in my stomach."

He belted out a laugh.

"Touché. Bonus points for colorful descriptions." He pointed at her seat belt, which was not secured across her body. "We're going off-road now so you might want to buckle up."

She pulled hard on the belt and latched it in, then continued. "One minute she's asking if I'm sweet on you—like I'm at some taffy pull with my Aunt Gertrude—and I no sooner get out the 'no way in hell' response when you show up and tongue thrust me into the next county! Out of thin air, I might add."

"That sounds so cold and clinical." He shifted gears on the truck as they drove across the property in search of the fences they were going to fix. "Not to mention painfully unromantic. I prefer to think of it this way: for some reason, the spirit moved me to kiss you. And when I kissed you, it felt so good and so right that I decided to see if you were enjoying it as much as I was. And usually when that happens, the kisser ventures into what could be hostile territory, but it's more like the kisser is hoping it's going to be friendly terrain."

"Are we talking war zone here or a make-out session?"

He grinned. "The way I see it, it kind of started like a war zone, but then it morphed into a make-out session."

She scrunched up her nose and buried her face in her hands. "Oh God. What have I done?"

"Um, you enjoyed a little kiss with me?"

She shook her head. "Yeah, but this"—she pointed at him then at herself—"is not okay. It's not good. It's weird."

He held up his hand. "If your goal was to chip away at my fragile male ego, you're succeeding."

"It's not you, it's me." She sighed.

"Wait a minute. Didn't I hear Zoey say you came here

to meet me? You were all set on some grand romance with the ring man, weren't you? And now it's wrong?"

"Yeah, but I realized that was stupid. And then, well, everything went all off the rails with us, and so it's like, it's not right."

He shook his head. There was no reasoning with this woman at the moment. He'd have to devise a better strategy. In the meantime, it was time to mend some fences. Perhaps both literally and figuratively.

Chapter Eleven

IZZY was so glad they got to the first break in the fence so they could redirect the conversation to something a little less tetchy. Or at least a little more user-friendly for her purposes. She hopped out of the cab, not even waiting for Sully to come around and help her out. The less physical contact, the better at this point. She knew this because she was unwilling to admit even to herself how much that kiss affected her. Yikes. The minute his mouth was on hers felt like a revelation. Like there was every other guy she'd ever kissed, and then there was Sully's kiss, which felt like it was the first time and the thousandth time and each time was better than the time before.

He surprised her immensely when he went from tame to all in as he had. The minute his tongue slid into her mouth, she had it bad. Way bad. Like she was hard-pressed not to imagine how much she wanted to do with that talented tongue of his—a tongue that left her wanting more. It didn't help matters that he looked so hot in his beat-up blue jeans and work boots and a T-shirt that fit tightly across his chest and his biceps and ugh, she had to gnaw on her fingers to stop the image from further distracting her.

Sully climbed up into the back of the pickup and tossed down a bunch of tools she supposed were necessary for the task at hand while Blizzard ran around and chased blowing grass and butterflies, barking as if it was his job.

"So, is this what we need to conduct the delicate fence surgery?" She winked at him and lowered her voice to sound like an announcer. "We can rebuild him."

"Are you seriously quoting from *The Six Million Dollar Man*?"

"I don't know why, but my mother used to always say that to me if I broke something when I was a kid. She'd try to make light of it so I wouldn't get upset."

"Your mom sounds like a sweet woman."

"She's awesome. The best. When I was a little girl I figured she was my playmate. We had so much fun together. Still do. My father left her when I was a baby, so it was only the two of us. And for my whole life, she's been my number one cheerleader."

"I'd love to meet her sometime," he said as he grabbed a shovel and handed it to Izzy along with a pair of work gloves.

She tried to imagine what it would be like to bring her mother out here to Montana to meet Sully. Like if they were girlfriend and boyfriend and they dated and after a while it was time to meet the parents. Which made her realize she hadn't met the parents of the last several guys she dated. How bad was that? She couldn't even get past what might be considered the first base of relationships: family introductions.

She glanced over at Sully who was speaking to her, much to her own oblivion.

"So, this post is down here," he said, pointing at what was obviously a post that got knocked down by something, considering it was lying on the ground. "We have to remove the base of the post that is still in the ground." He handed her one of the shovels and grabbed the other one. "It's going to require some elbow grease, but the good news is you've got some crazy sexy biceps on you that tells me you work out religiously at the gym, so I'm sure it'll be a breeze." He gave her a sly wink.

Crazy sexy biceps, eh? He was right. She spent an inordinate amount of time at the gym. Sometimes it was to scout out men she could date—yeah, sad to admit that. But she worked hard to get the physique she had and she was flattered he'd noticed. Now to prove her biceps justified the gym membership.

She started digging, pushing the spade into the soil right at the edge of the post, but it was not budging.

"You could try shoveling in toward the side of that buried post, and get the point in there to use it as a lever to pop it out."

Well, wasn't he clever? She took his advice and dug down at an angle and voila—it lifted right out.

"Now we need to make space to put the replacement post in." Sully held up a long, large tool that looked like something you might use as a torture device. "This is called a post-hole digger, and with your hands together up here, you dig it in, then do this to open it up."

Wow—it worked surprisingly well. This was going to be much easier work than she thought.

Next Sully helped her measure replacement posts and rails, and he cut them to size with a chainsaw he'd brought along.

"You put the post in, line it up with the rail, put in dirt at the base of the post, then pack it hard with this rubber mallet."

"Wow, how'd you learn to do stuff like this?"

"I grew up on a farm out in the country in southwest Virginia," he said. "I learned early on to help with chores like this. Farm life isn't easy, and everyone needs to chip in to manage it well."

"How many of you were there?"

"I was one of four kids. My mother taught school and my father worked construction. They ran the farm in their off-hours."

"So you *did* learn the value of a hard-day's work."

"And then some," he said. "I got to where I am by working my ass off. So that now I don't have to work my ass off. Unless I feel like it. Case in point." He spread his arms out around them.

"Yeah, well, you'd be one of the few men I know who is hardworking."

"Ouch."

She shook her head. "That's probably unfair. I'm sure there are guys I know who work their butts off, but the ones who linger in my mind tend to be the standouts with laziness. Or maybe it's annoyingness that I'm conflating with laziness."

"Annoyingness? I didn't even know that was a word."

"If it's not, it should be."

He pulled out his phone and entered the word into a dictionary app. He shook his head. "Well, I'll be damned, you're right. It is a word."

"It was inevitably going to become a word considering there are probably enough women in the world annoyed with the chronic annoyingness of the men in their lives."

"So what happened to the last guy you dated?"

She laughed a half laugh. "Dating might be a stretch. I mean yeah, we were together for a few months, but all the effort came from me. His efforts were concentrated on making sure he watched as many football games in a four-day period as possible. There wasn't room in his life for football and me." She groaned. "But then I have to be honest about this. He was so not for me. For instance, he had this small penis vehicle—a big ole pickup truck."

Sully lifted a brow and looked over at his enormous pickup nearby.

Izzy slapped her hand over her mouth. "Oh crap. I didn't mean it like that. I mean, well, you've got a truck because you need a truck. You're driving off-road and you're hauling tools and you probably do things like kayaking and camping and stuff, so you have a need. See, HR guy—"

"HR guy?"

She hung her head. "Yep. Cliché, no? Hooking up with a guy from the office? Anyhow, HR guy had this penis-compensation vehicle, a huge pickup, the kind with the big wheel hubs that make it that much harder to park in a city parking lot, right? And the thing is, it's not like he needed it. No one who lives in LA needs such a massive truck except a guy who is compensating. Or if he hauls trash for a living."

She continued yapping away about HR guy for a few minutes but noticed things had gone silent. She looked up to see Sully standing in front of her. He'd taken off his shirt, and for a minute there, Izzy wanted nothing more than to lick the sweat glistening off his tanned chest. He reached out and tucked a hank of her hair behind her ear.

"I'm not sure if I shouldn't do what I did before, but to be fair, this time I'm going to ask you."

His eyes fixed on her icy-blue ones, and they stood there for what seemed like minutes.

"Permission to come aboard, Captain?"

If only he meant that in the literal sense. She stared at him for a beat longer, then nodded ever so slowly.

He reached over and softly placed his finger beneath her chin, pulling her face gently toward his own. When they were a mere hairbreadth away from each other, he said in a soft whisper, "Now that I've got you where I want you, I have to ask: may I kiss you with my tongue?"

Which was a question she'd never had anyone pose to her, but he'd done it with such gentlemanly intent, well, hell, what was she to say? Hell to the yes? Hell yeah.

She didn't want to appear too overly zealous, so she instead slowly opened her mouth and angled her head to meet his mouth with her own. The minute their mouths met, she melted into his body. It could have been the heat, or it could have been his heat. Or it could have been that she wanted to get closer to that tanned, slick chest of his to map all the lines and contours of his beautiful torso with her fingers. If she was going to hell for her stupidity, she might as well enjoy it on the way down.

Chapter Twelve

SULLY had indeed removed his shirt because he was hot. As a bonus, she clearly got turned on seeing him in the nude from the waist up. His one regret was that he had no way to get her in the same condition. He'd have to settle for what he could get. Which right now meant a command performance of what happened back at Eleanor's house, only this time with intent on both sides.

He heard a soft thunk and looked over to see Izzy had let her shovel fall to the ground. God he'd love to have that be the two of them falling to the ground and scrabbling to remove each other's clothes. But he had to take things slowly with her, so instead he was savoring the moment as his tongue slid along the smooth surface of her straight, white teeth, then delved farther into her mouth to find her tongue probing for his, then stroking his tongue with long, slow swirls. Sully couldn't stop himself from letting out a long, low moan as Izzy reached out and ran her hands across his chest, dragging them along his torso, stroking from beneath his arms down to his waist, teasing him with fingers that could so easily slip beneath the edge of his waistband.

All he could hear was the whisper of wind in the trees and the gasping sounds coming from Izzy, who was pressing closer to him like a cat in heat. That was fine by him. He took advantage of her obvious pleasure to let his fingers explore a little, first with them settled at the base of her back, where he slid his fingertips beneath the waistband for a test run of what she was willing to consider.

When that seemed to elicit no objections, he pulled her toward him, pressing her ass as he did so. It was clear she could feel his arousal—it was impossible not to—and he wanted her to know how having her warmth pressed up to him turned him on. He ground his crotch against her center and she groaned. God, what he would give to drop everything and bend her over by the cottonwood tree and fuck her here and now until she screamed his name out while climaxing. But he couldn't do that—not yet. They barely knew each other. Not that it hadn't stopped him in the past. But this seemed different... like he needed to go slow and treasure each step along the way.

His hands crept toward the front, sliding beneath her T-shirt and skimming over her tight abs, then covering a breast with each palm as she moaned out his name. Soon his fingers began to pinch and tweak at her nipples beneath the cups of her bra, and she pressed her pelvis even firmer against his cock. He'd have to will himself not to go off in his jeans. They had more fences to repair and then lunch with Eleanor, so the last thing he wanted was a big old wet spot by his crotch. But that didn't mean he couldn't do her the favor...

One hand slipped away from playing with her nipples and slid down her soft belly, unbuttoned the top button of her jeans, and unzipped them. His fingers made short work of traveling down beneath the edge of her underwear—a veritable miracle he'd even gotten access—and slipped between the slick lips of her pussy. He stroked along them and circled her clit as her breathing became labored. Deepening the kiss, she spread her legs to give him better access.

Sully moaned into her mouth at the feel of her wet

center, and when he slid two fingers inside of her, he thought he'd died and gone to heaven. He continued to pinch and tweak her nipple, which had grown hard with desire, and he slicked his fingers through her pussy faster and faster. The pace of her breath, the firm grip on his ass as she pressed him toward her even harder told him everything he wanted to know: she was close to coming. He plunged a third finger inside her, pressing the flat of his palm against her clit as he went deeper and pulled out.

"Oh God, Sully, don't stop. I'm coming—" she moaned out loud, only to be echoed by the mournful moans of Blizzard, who joined in solidarity to the cause.

Sully pressed deep inside her as she climaxed, the muscles of her pussy spasming around him. He so wished that was his cock right now, but with a bit of luck—and strategy—it would be. And he was going to try his damnedest to make sure it became a reality.

In the meantime, his cock was as stiff as a fence post, and they had plenty more of them to repair before lunchtime, so his hard-on would have to wait its turn.

Chapter Thirteen

WHAT'S the standard protocol for when you're out in a field in the middle of nowhere fixing fence posts and the hot guy next to you ever so kindly decides to treat you to an orgasm? Because that was one hell of a climax. Made Izzy rethink the notion of living in rural America. To hell with city life if this was what you did all day out here. Shame they had more posts to fix. She'd have liked nothing more than to plant his pole in a particularly memorable place.

Not that she was going to do that, mind you. She had already decided that this guy was off-limits. Not the least of which was because of the droves of desperate women (yeah, yeah, she might have fit into that very category when she came racing up to Bristol, but she'd had a change of heart) willing to do anything to get a piece of him. Meanwhile, she was trying to figure out if moaning in ecstasy to the accompaniment of a howling dog was weird or not. Simpatico or downright weird?

Right now though, hmmm. How do you segue from that—screaming-hot orgasm—to not that? She stood there regaining her breath as she pondered the awkwardness of the situation. Luckily he was on it and reached for her hand.

"We've got a few more of these to fix before lunch, so we'd better get a move on." He threw her a sly look.

They collected their tools, putting them back into the bed of the truck, then hopped into the cab to drive on.

Two hours of sweaty, hot labor passed with easy conversation between them. It wasn't like Izzy to want to be outside shvitzing like a racehorse, but this felt both comfortable and gratifying. The benefits of a workout at Wild Card West Boxing minus the ubiquitous overpriced Lululemon-wear.

At last, Izzy had the nerve to get to the meat of the matter. "Do you mind if I ask you something?"

He shrugged as he stooped over positioning a rail back into place. "Fire away."

"What made you do this big ring giveaway contest?"

He stood up. "Well, I guess it seemed like a good idea." He reached into his back pocket and pulled out a bandana and mopped his damp brow. Izzy was having a hard time not focusing on his sweat-glistened chest as he spoke. Now that she'd had her hands on it, she was itching for a command performance. Yet considering she was conflicted about pursuing anything amorous with him, she wasn't about to take the lead.

She half smiled. "Yeah... So living on kale and protein smoothies with almond milk seems like a good idea too, but in reality, not so much."

He laughed. "That doesn't even remotely sound like a good idea to me. Now if you'd have said a steady diet of banana splits and pizza, I'd be totally on board with that."

She nodded. "You and me both."

"But getting back to this thing that has gotten a little out of control... I spent a year mired in misery after Gretchen left me. I took it so personally. Not only was I sad to have lost this woman I loved and thought I wanted to spend my life with, but my feelings were badly bruised. I pouted around and wrote sad songs and sang sad songs and worked through my angst by having a succession of one-night stands with women I chose because I'd never have to deal with them again. It was much easier that way than it was confronting my emotions." He scrunched his nose. "I am a guy, after all. We aren't often known for addressing those deeper issues."

"Okay so you were a bit of a male ho, I get that, but that's still a far cry from the ring giveaway."

He held up his hands. "Be patient. I'm getting to that." He'd moved on to the next fence post and had finished filling it with dirt and hammering it down. "You go ahead and supervise while I do the hard work." He winked at her.

"You're doing such a fine job. And, well, the view from here sort of precludes much more action."

He nodded toward the mountains. "It truly is God's country."

She looked up. "Ha! I wasn't talking about the mountains. I was talking more about what was directly in front of me."

He squinted. "You like what you see?"

"I'd be a fool not to."

He nodded. Funny how he didn't choose to seize on that and instead carried on the conversation. Of course Izzy could have taken the moment to make a move, too, but she was too much of a wimp. Even though her libido was coaxing her despite her better judgment.

"So I discovered that after a while it gets boring being whiny." He dusted off his gloved hands as he spoke. "And extremely unfulfilling. I knew I had to make a break from the past and move the hell on." He looked off toward the mountains. "And I knew that ring was not going to play any part of my life anymore. Not as if I'd use it if I ever got engaged again—bad juju to keep it with me. But with someone else, it could have a new life, especially if a good message was attached to it. So I figured giving it away was the best option." He scuffed the dirt with the tip of his boot.

"The thing is, how do you give away a nearly hundred-thousand-dollar ring?" he continued. "I wanted someone who wanted to get married, someone who couldn't necessarily pony up the money even for something small but significant. Someone who would really treasure this thing that I'd grown to see as symbolic of failure in my life. You know what they say—one man's trash is another man's treasure. Well, despite its cash value, it was kind of trash for me, but I knew it was certainly treasure for pretty much anyone else on the planet. So how do I find the right person to grant this fairy godmother wish to?"

She tapped her chin. "I can see your dilemma. It's not like you want someone who's going to hock it on eBay to get it."

"Yep. And what is the best way to get the greatest reach these days?" He pointed in the air. "Through social media. It seemed so obvious to me. Put it up there, make it a short time period so as to not draw out the whole process, and be done with something that no longer needs to be in my life."

Wow. What a good guy he is. Why would she have not given the man the benefit of the doubt? He was so darned normal and simply wanted to do something nice and put it out there in the world. And here she was giving him a rash of shit for, well, dog doo that probably wasn't even his dog's. Because it was clear he was not the type of guy who'd do that.

"So, have you received a crazy amount of replies?"

He heaved a sigh and nodded. "An insane number. Last time I checked there were around fifteen thousand emails. *Fifteen thousand!* I don't have time to go through that many emails! And trust me, none of them are short. They're long, detailed stories about their loves, their lives, their dreams. All good stuff, but geez, I evidently didn't think this through."

"I'll say. So what about getting help with all this? Like organize a reading party, where you divide up the emails with everyone in attendance. Surely there are easy ones to discard. Narrow it down to the final ten or twenty. Everyone reads those and votes on it. Maybe you can get the whole town involved. I mean, you need the ones reading the emails to be people you trust, but then for the final vote, get everyone together to cast their ballots. Like maybe on a private Facebook group or something."

He cocked his head and looked at her, grinning. "You're kind of a genius. Where do you come up with these ideas?"

She shook her head. "I'm a reformed publicist," she said. "Worked at it for years until I got tired of being a publicity whore. It started feeling kind of cheap always pushing stuff on people. I do recognize the value in the work—helping people to broadcast their message in the most effective way. But on a day-to-day basis, I was badgering media outlets for coverage over dumb things that wore on me. I mean, how many times can you beg a local newspaper to write a story about a restaurant's new line of scented cocktails? I got tired enough of it a few months ago to take a little sabbatical from my job. I've been living on a nice chunk of money that my grandmother generously left to me when she passed away a few years ago." She stooped over to help Sully line up the final rail. "But this—I mean this is kind of perfect, isn't it?"

"Beyond genius. Now if you could figure out how to get these women off my back." He thrust out his lower lip in a pout.

"You don't like being the poster child for virtue, humanity, and decency?"

He shook his head. "I don't like women throwing

themselves at me shamelessly. I mean, would they do this to me if I hadn't done this ring thing? Hell no."

Izzy thought perhaps she might throw herself at him if she'd first seen him singing at Harry's. He had a beautiful voice and his words resonated with her deeply.

"Part of me is like 'where were you all when I was a fifteen-year-old boy and wanted women throwing themselves at me?'" They both laughed at that.

"It's true. I mean I know musicians have groupies but damn, when you were taking that break at Harry's, the women were shameless. It was a bit of overkill."

He nodded. "That's putting it mildly."

"Kudos to you for not taking advantage of it. I guess in their own way, those women are sort of sad and vulnerable, and you are kind of like the white knight to them."

He pursed his lips. "I have no interest in being anyone's white knight. I'm your average guy and want to be treated as such."

"In that case, Mr. Average, can we get out of here and go have lunch? I'm starving and don't want to stay here, or I might be accused of fawning over you. God forbid you misconstrue me as a ring groupie."

Even though that was the original genesis of her being in town right now, it was that very thing she now shunned. She figured she'd keep that bit to herself for safekeeping.

Chapter Fourteen

"AH, Eleanor, you're a gem of a woman." Sully rubbed Eleanor's shoulders in gratitude as they sat down to a lunch she'd made especially for them, including chicken salad—from fresh chickens she'd raised on the ranch—and homemade croissants, which to Sully seemed like something that only happened in a dream. His mother was a talented baker and he warmly remembered those days he'd come home from school to fresh-from-the-oven bread and homemade butter and jam. This brought back the fondest of memories, and since Eleanor was almost like a mother to him, it was fitting. He took a seat on the porch, flanked on either side by the two women.

"Speaking of gems, what gives with that ring of yours?"

"Ugh, that ring has become an eight-headed hydra," he said. "But Izzy, here, has come up with a brilliant plan to figure this all out. Because if it were left up to me, it would take ten years to get through all the submissions I've received so far."

Eleanor lifted up her glass of tea toward Izzy. "I could tell she was a keeper from the minute I met her," she said, smiling.

Weirdly Sully could almost tell that too. Once he sifted through her rage issues, that is.

"Oh, Eleanor, you're too kind, but believe me, I'm not any great shakes."

But when she shook that cute little ass of hers... *ay yai yai* how that got to him.

"She's being humble, isn't she?" Eleanor winked at Sully.

"No, I'm being serious. To be honest, when I first met Sully, I hated him."

Eleanor laughed. "That's always the best sign."

"Hate at first sight?"

"All on the same continuum, my dear," she said as she took a bite of her sandwich. "You'd rather that than complete ambivalence. You can't do anything about someone who is neutral about you. But if you inspire some extreme in temperament, then you've got a relationship in play."

"In that case, we're practically engaged," Sully blurted out with a laugh. Izzy gave him a side kick on the ankle.

"I'm serious," Eleanor said as she lifted the pitcher and refilled everyone's tea. "The first time I met Jed was at a horse show in a nearby town. His horse stepped on my foot and broke a toe. Jed insisted that his horse had done nothing of the sort, but I gave him a piece of my mind. So, he took me back to his barn to tape up my toes and the next thing you know we were up in the loft and we kissed. Before I knew it we were rolling around in the hay bales and, well, the rest is history. We ended up eloping only a month afterward. Of course back then if you were young and randy and you wanted to have sex you got married, so what can I say? But we were on to something because we were married for forty-five years and raised five wonderful children together." Her eyes twinkled with mischief as she tore off a piece of her sandwich to give to Blizzard.

"Why, Eleanor Mullaney if you' aren't are a sassy thing!" Sully poked her in the ribs.

She nodded. "I'm telling it like it was. Everyone likes to think things were different back then, but they weren't a whole lot different than they are today. Boys and girls, men and women, they fall in love, and sometimes they fall in hate first. It's what you do with it that matters."

Sully pondered that notion for a minute, and realized she was spot-on.

As Sully and Izzy drove the final post into the ground, the late-afternoon sun blazed a trail of warmth and the colors of a Bellini cocktail painted the sky. When he looked at the glowing landscape he was continually reassured that moving to Bristol was the smartest thing he'd done in ages. Sure it wasn't the best for sustaining a relationship with his affianced. But who knew that at the time? And if he needed to be here and she couldn't be, then how could they have continued anyhow? One or the other would have been unhappy, and that wasn't right. Although not like he could expect to carry on a relationship with Izzy, who was also a city girl from the other side of the country. Shame he couldn't find someone local who wanted to remain here. But he figured at least he'd try to play things out with Izzy and see where it took him. Definitely not to LA. He and Blizzard would hate that.

He shook his head—talk about premature thinking. How weirdly optimistic of him after a year of pessimism about relationships.

"So, uh, who knew ole Eleanor was a bit of a horndog in her youth?" He lifted his eyebrow as he gazed into Izzy's blue eyes. He could probably get lost in those eyes if he let himself. Or if she let him. Was she even willing to do that?

"Right? I was sitting there thinking about Ellie and Jed up in the loft, making all sorts of noises and then coming back down covered in hay, sticking out of her braid and stuff."

"She's quite the motivational speaker, isn't she?"

"You mean in encouraging sexual congress early on in a relationship?" Izzy laughed.

"Sexual congress… It sounds like you need to gavel the meeting to order before proceeding."

"Would be far better than the congress we're all stuck with."

"You're not kidding. But let's not talk about greedy old men who fail to do the job they were hired to do. Let's discuss the good type of sexual congress, rather than the useless one."

"I'm all ears."

"So, right now, I'd love to take you up into Eleanor's barn and have my wicked way with you, but I'm not sure you're ready for that." He grinned and cocked his brow. "But as a plan B, what say you and I take the day tomorrow and get to know each other a little better? I'd love to take you out riding if you're up for it."

"Riding?" She squinted at him.

"Horses, silly. Maybe if you're lucky I'll show you my own barn." He winked. "But seriously, we'll make a day of it. You can help me groom and saddle them up, and I'll show you exactly why I upended my life and moved to this little slice of heaven here in Montana."

"I've never stepped foot on a horse in my life, Sully."

"Well, then, that's good—no bad habits to break. Because you should never step foot on a horse, anyhow."

She laughed. "I'm serious. I would hardly know the

head from the tail. Besides, they kick don't they?"

"I can assure you, my Missy is a lover, not a fighter. Kind of like her owner. She'll treat you like a lady. Kind of like her owner."

Izzy shook her head. "I'm convinced you are too good to be true, Sully Forester. I can't promise I'm going to be great at getting on—and staying on—your Missy, but I'm game if you are."

He grabbed hold of the belt loops of her jeans and pulled her toward him.

"I'm starting to think I'm game for anything that involves you." He leaned forward and pressed his lips to hers, then pulled her tighter for a kiss. The warmth of her mouth, still tasting vaguely of hibiscus tea, made him groan. He could so get used to this. His hands swept across her back and finally tucked into the waistband above that amazing ass of hers, and he pressed her toward his swollen cock. Damn, he was going to have to go home and take care of that ASAP as soon as he could extricate himself from kissing and touching this vexing woman.

Izzy slid her hands up along his chest, massaging his pecs and tracing her hands along his sides. She moaned into his mouth and he deepened the kiss, his tongue stroking along hers. In the distance, he could hear a car slowing along the road, but, too preoccupied with the business at hand, he paid no attention to it.

The next thing he knew, the whirring sound of a camera along with a succession of clicks, one after another, echoed in the background. Blizzard—off chasing imaginary prey— at last came racing toward the sound, barking loudly.

Izzy broke the kiss and looked over her shoulder as Sully glanced that way as well, to see a man hanging out the window of a large black SUV, snapping away at them. He paused, gave them a thumbs-up sign, snapped a few more shots, and drove away.

What the ever-loving fuck? Paparazzi? In the middle of nowhere? In this pristine land he called home? Great. Fucking marvelous. Right when he thought things were starting to look up.

Chapter Fifteen

"OH my God," Izzy said. "I mean seriously. Oh my God. What was that all about?"

He looked at her with a sheepish grin. "My fifteen minutes of unwanted fame, coming to a theater near you?'

"You're not kidding." She sighed. "Look, Sully, that's a little more than I was bargaining for. Who the hell knows what they're going to do with that picture. Imagine if that had been earlier today! I need to get back to Zoey's. This has been a bit too much."

Sully frowned. "But we were having a good time."

She nodded. "Yeah, I know. But now this—" She pointed down the road. "This makes things weird. I'm not sure what I want to think about that. It's not my scene, being anonymously photographed while I make out with a man I could easily have been in the middle of undressing."

Wait a minute, did I actually say that?

Sully's eyes opened wide. "You could have?"

She waved her hands as if erasing her words. "I mean in theory. I could just as likely have been at a coffee shop ordering a café Americano. It was a figure of speech."

Sully pursed his lips and nodded. "Gotcha. No intent behind it but kind of throwing it out there."

"Exactly."

"Okay, I'll take you back. As long as you keep your promise about tomorrow."

"I promised something about tomorrow?"

He nodded. "You sure did. We're going riding, remember?"

"Yeah, but I'm not sure about this now. I don't know that we should be seen together. It's going to arouse all sorts of suspicions."

Being with him had, after all, aroused all sorts of other things too, like her damned betraying libido.

"Impossible. We are going to be out where no one can find us. It'll be you, me, and Mother Nature."

"And by Mother Nature, do you mean what Eleanor described in the barn loft?"

He laughed. "I'll make no promises about loft action. I mean you and me in the great outdoors with whatever wildlife decides to make its presence known. And the other part of nature? We'll have to let that take its course." He paused and stared into her eyes. "Oh, and wear those boots."

"Oh my God, Izzy, I can't believe you were going at it with Sully! That's fantastic!" Zoey clapped her hands with glee. The two of them were sitting on the back deck, Snowball weaving figure eights between their legs as they sipped wine and watched the sun descend behind the jagged peaks of the Rockies. The setting was spectacular.

"I'm not sure about fantastic. I mean it's kind of weird. Because I came here with that delusional thinking that I'd swoop in and make him fall for me. And then I met him not knowing it was him and I hated the hell out of him. When we saw him at Harry's, I thought he was a bit of a jerk with all the women around him. I so dreaded spending the day with him, but it turned out to be quite awesome. He was sweet and thoughtful and hardworking and Eleanor was delightful and well, let's say he is good with his hands if you know what I mean."

Zoey's mouth dropped open. "You mean he got you off?"

Izzy's face warmed as she nodded. "Um, with precision skills, I might add."

"Oh man, imagine what it'll be like with his precision tool then."

Izzy's eyes grew wide. "I'm not going to sleep with him."

"Well, at some point you are, aren't you? I mean isn't that what happens in a relationship?"

"This isn't a relationship. This is a-a-a—"

"Relationship."

Izzy knit her brows. "No. I mean we went and worked together for the day."

"And you swapped spit. And you fondled his hard body. And he had his hands down your pants. I'd say two plus two plus two equals two—in other words, the two of you in a relationship." She winked at her.

"Can't this be a one-night stand? I mean a one-day stand?"

"Why would you settle for a one-off when you might be able to aspire to more?"

"Because he's got this crazy amount of rabid women on a mission to land him, for one thing."

"But he doesn't want them, Izzy. It sounds to me like you're the only one on his radar screen. Why don't you relax into it and enjoy the ride."

"Speaking of rides, I committed to going riding with

him tomorrow."

"Now that's a good girl." Zoey patted her hand. "Go do fun things with the man and see how much you enjoy each other's company. It's what people do when they're getting to know each other better."

Izzy knit her brows. "What if I don't want to get to know him better?"

Zoey wagged her finger at her friend as she took a sip of wine. "Ahhh, but you do. I've known you long enough—you're at least intrigued by him. And if nothing else, you wouldn't mind a try at that precision tool of his."

With a shake of her head, Izzy smirked. "Your mind is in the gutter, Zoey Richards."

"Takes one to know one." She refilled their wineglasses. "Now I want you to go tomorrow with an open mind—and possibly open legs—and report back to me about that precision tool of his."

Rolling her eyes, Izzy wasn't sure if it was wise to heed her friend's advice. But the idea was becoming more and more appealing with each minute she was away from Sully, left only to replay the events of the day and counting the minutes till she could go riding: with him or on him remained to be seen.

Chapter Sixteen

IZZY pulled up to the Circle XOXO Ranch and stared at the name of the place for a few minutes as Sully wandered up to greet her.

She pointed at the sign hanging over the entrance to his property. "Circle XOXO? Really?"

"It's kind of got a dual meaning," he said as he leaned in to kiss her gently. "First off, because, well, I love it out here. I love it to death. More than I ever knew I would. But yeah, also at first, the idea was that it was where she-who-shall-not-be-named and I were planning to start our married lives together. It seemed fitting."

"It was a sweet idea," she said. "Even if that bit didn't work out."

"But the rest did, big-time, so it's all good. Part of the journey, right?"

"Speaking of journey—I'm a little nervous about this. I've got zero experience on a horse."

"And Missy has zero experience with you on her, but that's fine. She's a sweet girl and gentle as a mama with a baby. You two will hit it off, I'm sure."

He hopped into her car as she drove back toward the house, parking in front of the barn, which was larger—and more pristine—than your average home.

Izzy leaned back as she looked up to take in the grandeur of the place.

"Well, I wanted a barn my horses would be happy in, and I was fortunate to be able to afford it," he said. "I had an architect come out and design something that was kind of modeled on the old Sears barns, but I let him take a lot of liberties with the design."

"Annnd you got a horse mansion. Nice."

"Whatever makes Missy happy. I like to keep the women in my life satisfied." He grinned. Maybe he was laying it on thick, but why not let Izzy know he liked her and was interested in exploring a relationship? Never could he have imagined finding his way back to a place where that mattered. For the first time in forever, he was excited about a woman, both emotionally and physically. Nothing wrong with that.

They entered the barn's interior—complete with polished tongue-in-groove oak ceilings with skylights and white beadboard wainscoting with chair railing lining the walls throughout.

"So I'm going to take you through the entire process to prepare for this ride. Every time I go out on my horse, Chunk, I do all of this. It's good to learn the proper way from the start."

"The only thing I know about horses I learned from Mr. Ed, one of my mother's favorite old TV shows," she said. "This will be quite an education for me!"

Sully chuckled and proceeded. "The first thing we do is tie up the horse to keep her from running scared." He secured a rope to the horse's chest and tied it to the wall. "Once that's in place, you want to brush the horse well to be sure all the dirt and grit is off of her—you don't want anything that'll irritate her underneath her saddle and cause chafing. If Missy starts getting sores from something rubbing wrong, she might misbehave on you—and I wouldn't blame her."

Izzy nodded. "Neither would I."

He handed her the brush and stood behind her, his front pressed to her back, and his hand led hers in stroking along the horse's hair. "Be sure to do it nice and easy, and get anywhere that saddle's gonna come in contact with her body."

They stood that way for a while, stroking in unison. Sully was tempted to stop what they were doing and get straight to the loft action, but it was premature for that.

Once he was satisfied Missy was brushed well, he started readying the saddle.

"You'll saddle from the left, and first we'll fold the saddle blanket in half, placing the fold to the front—positioning it forward, over the withers." He pointed to the area that was where the neck met the back. "Then slide it back into place. This keeps the hair flat on the back. Be sure the blanket is even on both sides and not wrinkled or folded, or it'll be uncomfortable for Missy."

He hooked the stirrups over the horn—to keep them from hitting either horse or him as he lifted the saddle—and raised it high enough to place it on the horse's back. "Be careful not to knock the blanket out of position after you've taken great care to place it right. And then we'll settle the saddle on her gently, so she's not spooked, placing it slightly forward and shifting it back."

He pointed to Missy. "Now I want you to check the pads for wrinkles. Make sure her hair is smoothed down. Don't be afraid to touch her—she likes it."

He pulled the stirrups down, then reached beneath the horse, grabbing the free end of the cinch.

"Now I'm cinching her gently, so she doesn't get upset. I'll wait for a minute till she exhales and tighten it a bit more.

Not too much—enough to hold the saddle in place firmly. You need to be able to slide your fingers between the cinch and the horse. You wouldn't want a corset binding you, and the horse doesn't want to feel that confined either."

He paused. The idea of Izzy in a corset was such a freaking turn-on he couldn't even go there or he'd never be able to mount his own horse.

Lastly he stood at Missy's head, facing back, and checked to be sure there were no wrinkles in the skin under the cinch.

"This is such a complicated process," Izzy said. "To think I assumed all you had to do was hop on the thing."

"It's all about doing it right so your horse is happy and comfortable. Now we're going to undo the halter, slide the noseband of the halter down over Missy's nose, and slip the crown back up over her ears. You stand beside her neck, facing forward, with the bridle in your left hand, then slip the reins over her neck. See how easy this is?" He smiled at her.

"It's kind of fun."

"Now comes the actual fun part. You get to slide the bit into her mouth."

"The mouth with those huge teeth that could make quick work of my fingers?"

"You'll be fine." He stood behind her and guided her. "So with your left fingers, move the bit against her lips and insert your thumb into that space between her front and back teeth. You might need to wiggle your thumb to encourage her to open her mouth wider, but Missy is usually cooperative. There you go. Now slide the bit in and lift the bridle higher with your left hand so she can't spit it back out. But don't pull too hard. Good job. Now pull the crown over Missy's left ear, gently bend her right ear forward to slip it beneath the crown, and pull that over her ear. Great work, Iz."

He helped her finish preparing the bridle and led her horse out of the stable, grabbing a helmet for her on the way out.

"Now it's time to get on top of her. You ready?"

Izzy pretended to nibble her fingernails.

"I'm as ready as I'm gonna be."

"Let's do it. Stand right here, next to Missy, holding the reins in your left hand with a little tuft of mane alongside the reins. Facing slightly forward, you're going to put your left foot in the stirrup—"

"The last time I had my feet in stirrups nothing good came out of it."

Sully stopped in his tracks to ponder that visual. "You're killing me here, Izzy. Here I'm trying to get you on a horse and you're talking about being spread-eagled naked in a doctor's office. This is not helping me right now."

She laughed. "Sorry. My bad."

He shook his head. "You are bad... As I was saying, your left foot is in the stirrup and you keep hold of the reins, then grab the horn and push up with your right leg, lifting it up and over the saddle."

He stood behind her with his hands on her butt and right thigh, trying hard to exorcise visions of her splayed wide at the gynecologist's office and trying harder not to notice that his hands had free rein over her butt and thighs. On the third attempt, she was up and in the saddle.

"Woot. I'm golden. Now when can we gallop?"

He laughed. "We'll work our way up to that. Let's take baby steps for now. That means making sure you're seated right on the saddle. You've got both feet in the stirrups now"—he closed his eyes and imagined that scenario again—"and your sit bones comfortably in the middle of the saddle seat, your legs hanging loose on each side." Jesus, never in his life had he been jealous of a saddle before, but damn if the saddle wasn't getting the best of things with her legs straddling it. "Don't slouch, but do be relaxed. Missy is your friend and she won't do you wrong. Your feet should lightly rest in the stirrups with the widest part of your foot, your heels angled slightly but not pressing down. Hold the reins in one hand while the other rests on your thigh. Some people like to rest it on the horn of the saddle. Hold your hands at an angle to the ground with your fingers closed around the rein in a relaxed fist. You might want to hold it between your baby and ring fingers."

"This is getting complicated! So many things to remember."

Sully clipped in his helmet and mounted Chunk in one swift move. He looked at Izzy next to him and smiled.

"You look like you belong there. And now you have to move! Gather your reins so you can feel a light contact with them. Use both lower legs to squeeze her lightly behind the cinch," he squeezed his legs together to show her. "Push forward slightly on your seat muscles to indicate to Missy you plan to move forward. Your hands should follow your horse's head as the neck naturally extends to move forward. As soon as she does what you tell her to do, stop cuing her. Once you start walking, enjoy the slight rocking with her pace and relax into it. Keep looking forward in the direction you want to go and keep your shoulders even with your arms relaxed at your sides and elbows slightly bent. There should be a straight line from your elbow to the bit and your reins should be fairly loose." He nodded at her as she followed his instructions.

"When you want to turn left, pull back with gentle

pressure on the rein in your left hand. Squeeze back rather than tug. Keep contact with the right rein too. As you're directing her to turn, apply some pressure with your left leg as that encourages her to turn in that direction. Again, once she obeys the cue, stop the pressure."

"I should've been taking notes."

"Not to worry. This will become second nature before you know it. It'll be exactly like riding a horse."

She laughed.

They started walking out into a pasture and continued on for a while until they got to a gate, where Sully pulled up alongside it, unlatching it and letting her pass through first before he closed it behind him. They walked through a cool forest, mostly in silence, taking in the sounds of nature, the breeze rustling the leaves, birds calling to one another, bees buzzing in the air.

Soon they could hear the burbling of water, and the forest gave way to a wide riverbank, where there were a handful of painted ponies drinking from the shallow waters.

"They're beautiful," she said as she watched them with concentration. "Whose are they?"

"They belong to a rancher whose property is up that way." He pointed across the river.

"They look like happy ponies."

"How could you not be, here?"

She nodded.

They walked for a while longer till they came to a clearing and a field filled with wildflowers.

Izzy gasped. "This is spectacular," she said. "Absolutely breathtaking."

"I'm glad you like it," he said. "Because this is where we're going to stop for lunch."

He tied up the horses and helped her down from

Missy's back, then got her to spread out the blanket with him.

As he retrieved the food from a saddlebag attached to Chunk, he turned to her. "You did a great job for your first time riding." He pulled out crackers and cheese and salami. Reaching into the bag, he extracted a bottle of champagne and two flutes.

"Sully—you spoil me! I might very well get used to this if you don't put the brakes on it."

"Well, that wouldn't be any fun to stop now, would it?"

Especially because he was only getting started.

Chapter Seventeen

IZZY had eaten plenty and was thoroughly satiated. She took another sip of her champagne and sprawled out on her back, staring up at the puffs of clouds scattered across the blue sky. They were surrounded by a field of flowers in shades of purples and blues and pinks and reds, in a field edged by deep, green, serene forests. Snow still capped the mountains on two sides and the gently burbling river was visible off to their right. This place was a slice of heaven on earth. She couldn't imagine how LA seemed more desirable than this, here, now.

Sully leaned next to her on his side, propped up on his left elbow, tickling Izzy's belly with a stem of lupine.

"What are you doing?" she said, looking down at the brilliant purple flower as it dusted her stomach.

"Just tracing a path where my tongue is going to go." He grinned at her.

"You think, do you?"

He leaned forward. "I don't think, I know." He rolled on top of her and started to kiss her all over her head and neck, making loud smacking sounds as he did it while tickling her sides with his fingers. Izzy laughed and protested without much intent behind it, but soon his playfulness turned serious and he leaned forward to kiss her. She dug her hands into his pockets as his hands framed her face, his tongue tracing along her lips, down to her jawline, and along her throat in that place that made her crazy with desire. She pulled him toward her, but he wiggled free and shifted, working his way down her body, nipping at her breasts through her shirt before he reached beneath her T-shirt and pulled it off, revealing a sexy black lace push-up bra.

"God, Izzy, now you're really killing me," Sully said as his tongue licked a trail down along her collarbone into the valley of her cleavage. He nudged away the cups of the bra to reveal pink nipples already beaded tight with anticipation. He traced his tongue along the areola of one breast while his fingers teased the other, pinching the nipple on one with his fingers while his mouth nipped and sucked and lathed the other.

Izzy writhed beneath him, her hips encouraging him with their message of yearning as she ran her fingers through his hair, enthusiastically pressing his head toward her. He switched sides, licking the other nipple and sucking hard as his free hand worked its way down her abdomen to unbutton her jeans and slide the zipper down with ease.

His hand shifted toward her hips, lifting the denim and jiggling it downward until she lent a hand and pulled as well. They came to a stop at her boots.

"Hmmm…" He paused to assess the situation. "What should we do about them?"

She gave him a sidelong glance. "Don't country girls do it with their boots on?"

He nodded. "That's what they say. But are you a country girl?"

"Not so much," she said, "but I'm a girl in the country if that counts."

He grinned. "It does indeed. In which case let's do this."

He sat up on his knees, staring down at her full, glorious breasts served up to him on the ledge of that sexy push-up bra, and it took his breath away. As his gazed traveled down her body, he saw for the first time the matching lace panties and he knew there was no time to waste. He needed a piece of that and he needed it fast. He pulled off one boot and then the other and dragged her pants down afterward, leaving her in those panties—but not for long—as he made quick work of them as well.

"Remember that thing about the stirrups?" He gave her a sly wink. "How's about we play a little doctor?"

She put her finger to her mouth and gave him a coy look. "Do you want me to tell you where it hurts?"

"I want you to tell me where it aches." He moved his body so that he was centered between her legs, which were spread wide now.

"Are you sure no one's going to come up here?" She glanced around to be certain they were still alone.

"I can promise you not a soul will show up. This is my property, darlin', and no one is coming on it without my express approval." He leaned down to inspect her pussy, which was already glistening with moisture. "I see what the problem is now." He slicked his finger through the wetness. "It looks like your pussy is in need of some TLC."

Leaning in, he stroked his tongue through her slick center and groaned at the sweet, salty taste of her. This was a flavor he would never tire of. He traced his tongue along her lips and around her clit, falling into a pattern that had her pressing her hips to his face at an accelerated pace. When he slid first one, then two fingers inside her moist channel, she moaned out loud. At the far end of the field, Blizzard, who had been tagging along all day, answered the call with his own howl of approval. They both laughed.

Sully moved the fingers of one hand up to her nipple while the fingers of his other played with her pussy and his

95

tongue stroked with greater intensity.

"Sully, please, I want to feel you in me when I come."

He shook his head. "Oh, no, baby. This is all you. Then we can worry about me."

"But I want to feel your hard cock in me when I climax."

"Not to worry, you'll do that too."

He pressed a third finger inside her, curving his fingers to hit that spot that he knew would send her over the edge, coupled with furiously tonguing around her clit. Izzy urged his face into her pussy and shouted out his name as her body convulsed in orgasm, her pussy spasming around his fingers and her juices flooding his mouth, making him moan. He gave her a minute to finish and quickly stripped off his clothes, rifling in his wallet for a condom, and rolling it on in record speed.

She pushed him over on his back and kissed her way down his torso.

"You put it on too soon, Sully," she said. "I wanted you to feel my warm, wet mouth on it."

Sully groaned. "What say you ride me like a true cowgirl and we'll save that for another day."

She cocked an eyebrow. "Boots or no boots?"

"We'll save them for another day too."

She lifted a leg over his hips and settled herself on his swollen cock, the head pressing into her wet opening as her body spread wide, taking him deep inside her. Once she pressed her pussy to his pelvis, she held still, with only a small little churn of her hips.

"More." He wasn't past begging if he had to. But he needed to feel the slide of her wetness along his cock while he watched her tits bounce as she thrust on him like she was holding on to a bronco for dear life.

He grabbed her hips as she started to raise them and helped guide them back down when his cock was almost out. The slick sound of his pounding into her wetness was all they could hear but for the whistling of the wind across the grasses and flowers. As he watched her grind her pelvis into him and draw it back again, teasing his cock with her body, Sully was intoxicated.

"Lean over," he said. "I need to suck on your tits while you do that."

Izzy obliged, guiding a nipple into his mouth as the two of them thrust against one another. It didn't take long for Sully to feel the pull of come, his balls tightening up, the twitch of muscles deep in his pelvis, as light and sound seemed to freeze momentarily and blast through his senses as he convulsed in orgasm. As Izzy's second climax erupted around him, his cock pulsed an endless stream of come and she collapsed on top of him, spent.

Boy, was he in deep, both literally and figuratively. Buried deep inside her and in deep emotionally as well. He had it and he had it bad. He only hoped Isabelle Strong could reciprocate.

Chapter Eighteen

IZZY was the first to wake up after what could only be described as the most arousing sexual experience of her life. What with her legs spread wide as the wind rustled through her pussy and his fingers, mouth, and cock worked their collective magic. Oh boy, was she in deep.

Sully was still snoring softly as she looked around and marveled at the sight of it. That's when she heard a snuffling, chuffing sound that was definitely not coming from Sully's mouth.

Blizzard, who had fallen asleep beside them, woke up and started to bark, which got Sully stirring as well.

"What is that?" Izzy said in a whisper, fully cognizant that they were in the wilderness stark naked and she had no idea what could be coming at them. Wolves? Panthers? *Do they have panthers out here?* She was holding out hope for something a bit more tame like a raccoon when she saw in the distance three bear cubs tumbling into the clearing, with a mother bear in tow.

"Oh my God! Look," she said, pointing at them. "This has got to be the best day ever."

"Listen, Iz, stay put, don't move. I'm going to tie up Blizzard, so he doesn't do anything impulsive, and I'll grab the bear spray in my bag in case we need it. You might want to slip on your clothes very slowly. But no sudden moves. We don't want the mama bear to even notice us if we can help it."

The bears were the distance of a football field away, which she'd hoped was a perfectly safe distance. She didn't even bother to put her clothes on, instead she lay on her stomach, transfixed by the graceful movements of the mama and the playfulness of the babies who were diving and swatting at each other and looked like they were having a great old time of it.

After a few minutes, the mama bear and her babies moved on in the opposite direction of Sully and Izzy.

Sully breathed a sigh of relief. "That was a little too close for comfort," he said, wiping his forehead with his hand. "I could see the headlines now: 'Naked Couple Mauled While Making Love.'"

Izzy's thoughts came to a standstill. Was that what this was—making love? Not merely having sex, but sex with some much deeper thing happening beneath it?

He came up behind her and lay on top of her, his belly pressed to her back, and she could feel him hardening against her.

"Oooh, why Mr. Forester, it seems that excitement in nature turns you on."

He leaned down and nibbled on her ear. "You, Ms. Strong, are what turns me on. Like nothing I've ever experienced before." He continued to lick and suck along her ear while lifting his hips then hers and reaching around to toy with her pussy, wet anew with need. In record time, he reached for his wallet in his pants nearby and removed the only other condom in there, slipping it on quickly and hitching her up onto her hands and knees.

"There's something so erotic about doing it doggy style out in the wild like this, isn't there?" He slid his cock inside her and held still.

"Why, I couldn't tell you as this is my first time like this."

"Mine too," he said on a forced breath, holding himself back. Finally he couldn't restrain anymore and grabbed her hips, withdrew, and thrust hard into her, repeating this again and again. "Reach down and rub yourself," he said. "I want to watch you bring yourself to climax while I fuck you from behind."

Izzy obliged as his hips drove into her and he plunged deep inside of her.

"Now, Sully," she rasped. "I'm about to come. Do it with me."

He gave it three fast thrusts as she moaned his name and her pussy clamped down on his cock, pulling the come from him in an eruption of pleasure that had him shouting out her name so loudly the neighbors could hear it. If there were any.

He lay there on top of her and an immense sense of satisfaction settled around her. This was where she was meant to be, with this man, and yeah, even with the moaning dog next to them.

"Next time, we're gonna need to lock Blizzard up somewhere," she said. "We're giving him ideas and not good ones."

Sully laughed. "Is this like the kids walking in on you?"

"Creepily so."

"We'll have to find a doggy eye mask or something. Or not bring him next time. Because trust me, there will be a next time for this. I've decided I'm a big fan of sexual congress in nature."

She smiled, as they rolled together laughing and relishing the moment.

"Sully! Honey! Baby! So great to see you!" A blond woman in a Lilly Pulitzer knock-off dress came running in high heels toward the barn. Izzy had just dismounted from her new best friend, Missy, who had treated her with kid-glove care today. Even though, yeah, her crotch was feeling a bit worse for wear and tear, between straddling a horse for hours and being ridden by a man a few times too. But those were good reasons for a little discomfort. But this—this beyotch gamboling toward them like a wobbly billy goat—Izzy didn't know what to make of her.

But she did pretty quickly when the woman jumped into Sully's arms and wrapped her legs around his hips—like what the ever-loving fuck was that all about? Evidently it wasn't a long-lost sister. Worse still, she started kissing him—with sounds and lips and moans as though she were auditioning for the role of worst kisser ever. Only it was in the arms—and on the mouth—of the man Izzy had spent an intimate afternoon with. No question about it, she wasn't a long-lost sister. Unless the man had a dark family history he'd failed to disclose.

Chapter Nineteen

SULLY stood stiff as a scarecrow as his ex-fiancée climbed all over him like a mad cat on a scratching post. It did not escape his attention that the woman he'd made love to moments ago stood nearby observing this relic from his past with great displeasure. It took some maneuvering—especially getting the woman's tongue away from his mouth, but he untangled himself enough to get her off him and find out what the hell was going on with her. Clearly she'd lost her mind. Or was on some kind of drugs. Or something.

He swatted at her like a cloud of gnats till at last, she stopped swarming him.

"What in the hell is going on, Gretchen?" He had that look on his face that you get when the dog won't stop barking after you've told it forty times to stop already.

"Baby, I've been thinking long and hard about things, and I think we should give it another go," she said as she ran her fingers through her hair trying to straighten out the muss that must've set in during her blind assault on Sully.

Sully squinted at her, trying to decipher what language she was speaking—it must've been some foreign tongue that made no sense to him. He could barely even muster up the words to say something to her.

"Huh?" was all he had in him.

"Oh, Sully, I heard all about your big contest and everyone back in New York is talking about what an incredible man you are and it made me start to think about what a great guy I gave up. And I saw that picture of you online and you were in some clinch pose like they have on romance novels—I don't know who it was clasping you as though you were her life preserver and without you she'd drown, but please, spare me that. So, I caught the next flight out. I know there are going to be women like that going after you and I felt the need to protect you from them."

Izzy had by now planted her feet solidly apart and placed her hands on her hips like that Wonder Woman power pose that was all in the news not too long ago, and Sully kinda liked it—it made her look badass, but he sobered realizing it had some alpha doglike meaning and she was probably pissed. Especially because he didn't have anything to do with this. He was blindsided by this bizarre attempt to capitalize on his awkward moment in the spotlight.

Picture... she mentioned a picture. What was she talking about? Oh, crap, that picture... Wait—that was taken yesterday! And it was already out there? Wow, things moved fast in the era of social media. Talk about an invasion of privacy.

"Um, would you mind elucidating matters regarding this picture you're talking about?"

She pulled out her phone and opened up a browser and pulled the picture up in seconds. Wow. So much for a life of privacy. There for the world to see and gawk at was a picture of a shirtless Sully, sweaty and not looking too bad all things considered, and Izzy, well, her hands were all over his chest and she looked like she had a personal stake in whatever was going on there, maybe owned some real estate across his torso. The second picture showed the two of them still hugging but peering at the photographer, Izzy glancing over her shoulder with a particularly deer-in-the-headlights stare.

Sully shook his head. "What the fuck is wrong with people?" He ran his fingers through his already bedheaded hair (or perhaps wildflower-field hair). He could not believe how his worlds were suddenly intersecting and not in a great way, all because he tried to do something nice. What a lesson he was learning. Nice was for idiots.

He heard footsteps and glanced over to see Izzy walking toward her car. She gave a halfhearted wave. "Catch you later." Sully tried to stop her, but she was backing up and out the driveway before he could do anything. Which left him standing alone with his ex who quite frankly he had no interest in ever running into again on a good day. Today? He wished he could press rewind and make her go away before he'd ever seen her.

It took a good hour or so before Sully could persuade Gretchen that even on a cold day in hell he wouldn't take her back. That Gretchen and Sully were a thing of the past. They had some good times together, they had some bad times together, and now they would have no times together.

"So, does that mean you aren't interested?" She tried one more time. He shook his head. "Can I stay the night at least? We can cozy up by the fireplace. Maybe I could try on the ring for old times' sake. It could be fun!"

Sully got up and went to the door and opened it as wide as it would go, then pointed outside. "Sorry, Gretchen. But it's time to say goodbye for good."

Chapter Twenty

"YOU do know Sully's a stand-up guy," Tanner said as Izzy wept over her fourth glass of wine. "I'd trust him with my life."

"Yeah, but would you trust him with your ex-wife? Or fiancée? Whatever she is. Was. Is."

"I'd be willing to bet money that the Sully Forester I know has already ushered her out the door and asked her not to return. It took a while for him to get over the relationship, but the last thing he's going to do is drop everything and go running back into her arms."

Izzy shook her head. "Yeah, because she already did that to him."

"Gretchen's not a bad person, she's just kind of—"

"Bossy?"

Tanner nodded. "Yeah, I'd say that."

"And bitchy?"

He shook his head. "With all due respect, I'm not gonna touch that with a ten-foot pole. I'll leave that to you ladies to duke out."

"You're a mensch, you know that Tanner Eliasson? Zoey's the luckiest girl in the world."

Zoey walked back into the room and lifted an eyebrow. "I am awfully lucky that Tanner and I found each other—or refound each other. Don't write Sully off. I think there's something there with you two."

Izzy started crying again. "I know there's something there. We fit together like a hand and a glove."

"Ahhh, drunken clichés. My favorite." Tanner grinned at Izzy.

"Don't laugh at me," Izzy said, swilling her wine. "I mean it. I was all set to not deal with him, but he broke down my defenses and then I even slept with him—I *slept* with him—and now what?"

Tanner and Zoey shot each other a look of surprise, their mouths forming matching Os.

"Oh, Izzy that's great news!"

"It *was* great news," Izzy said through sobs. "Better than great. But now look."

The doorbell rang and Tanner went to answer it.

"Dude, what the hell took you so long? Your girlfriend is marinating in zinfandel right now." He led him and Blizzard inside and into the living room, where they had a crackling fire going. Even in the summertime, the nights could get cool enough to justify it. Tanner's Labrador Suki leapt up as soon as she saw her friend Blizzard and they took off down the hallway to play.

Sully walked to the sofa where Izzy was curled up in a ball wailing. He reached for her and wrapped his arms around her, and even down the hall, Blizzard pitched in with his own empathy howl. Everyone but Izzy laughed.

"Hey, Iz." Sully reached for her chin with his pointer finger and lifted her head to look at him. Izzy didn't think she had it in her for this conversation right now. "I'm sorry that happened this afternoon, but I want to explain everything to you."

Izzy bawled through her tears. "I know, I know, she wants you back and you're gonna give it a go."

He knit his brows. "Do you think that little of me that

I'd do that? Especially right when our friendship is starting to form into something meaningful—or at least I hope it is!"

Drawing in a long breath, Izzy exhaled loudly. "I'm confused and need some space," she said at last. "I'd like to take a few days to think about things and then I'll let you know where I stand. Okay?"

Sully gave her a tight hug. "Take all the time you need. You know where to find me. I'll be waiting for you when you're ready, okay?"

She nodded. "Bye, Sully." She motioned with her eyes it was time for him to leave her be.

"It's not goodbye, Iz. It's a see ya later."

But she wasn't so sure about that. Dealing with this man who was now larger than life seemed to be more than she wanted to bargain for.

Chapter Twenty-One

SULLY was bleary-eyed. He'd spent the better part of the last four days pouring through thousands of email petitions from people who hoped to be the lucky winner of the engagement ring he couldn't wait to unload. He was keeping himself especially busy because during those four days he'd had no contact with Izzy, which was making him crazy. Also making him crazy were the nineteen thousand emails. Never in a million years did he think that many people at one point in time were thinking of getting married. Who knew?

Of course there were still so many to go through, which is why he'd arranged for Harry's to cater the official reading party he'd scheduled for this evening. It felt like half the town was coming to help him and for that, he was beyond grateful. Otherwise he'd probably have chosen some random prize generator online, though that seemed particularly impersonal and he was sure he'd miss out on the special person that way.

He was hoping Izzy would show up but it was anybody's guess. He'd texted both Zoey and Tanner in the hopes that they'd peer-pressure her to attend. He was willing to play dirty if it meant he'd have a chance to try to work things out with her.

He was still a bit mystified why she freaked out so much about Gretchen's little maneuver, but then again, the timing couldn't have been much worse. If only she'd felt like she was number one, instead of somehow thinking she was knocked down ten pegs by Gretchen's arrival. Crazy that he wouldn't realize how much he enjoyed being with her. And under her. And on her. And in her.

Everyone was told to bring some digital device along to access Sully's email server and read letters. They were going to read emails in rounds—each person in the room would take one, the person next to them would take the next one, and so on. They'd read, and read fast, then move on to the next one. There would be no time for messing around. It was like speed dating only even more impersonal.

The doorbell rang and people started arriving. Each time it rang, Blizzard felt compelled to announce it, so the noise level was ear-splitting. Sully was gonna have to do some sort of bark-howl training with that boy sometime soon. In the meantime, he would provide some amusement while everyone hunkered down to sort through the applications. With a bit of luck, they'd have it narrowed to a winner tonight.

Sully saw Tanner and Zoey enter hand in hand and he got his hopes up until Tanner glanced at him and shrugged, which he knew meant he tried to no avail to get Izzy here, darn it. So disappointing. He heaved a sigh and decided he needed to attend to his guests—at least it would keep him occupied. He wandered a little aimlessly around the spacious living room making small talk. The dramatic vaulted ceilings and walls of windows showcased the cobalt twilight that was settling in. A brilliant full moon tinged orange and cast low in the sky seemed to swallow up the horizon.

As people settled in to get to work, Sully rang a dinner bell to draw their attention.

"Okay, everyone," he said. He looked around the room

and did a loose head count. "Wow, great, we've got at least a hundred people here. This will help it go much faster. I think I'm going to change things up a bit so we can be more efficient, and starting with Angie to my right, each person will claim twenty emails to start. Angie, you name your ten at the top of the list and tag the person next to you, who will claim ten, then tag the person next to them, and so on. I don't know any way to make this easier, but that way we can go through a round before having to assign another set to everyone and we can avoid overlap. The last person to be assigned a grouping then tags me, so I know where we start with the next round. When you're done, come up to the front and we'll start round two. Anybody have any questions?"

He heard a rumbling coming from the back of the room as someone seemed to be working their way toward where Sully stood. Everyone else faded away as Sully saw Isabelle Strong approach him. He nodded at her, not sure what to expect.

"You have a question for me before we begin?"

She darted her eyes around the room and toed the floor with her cowboy boots.

"So, I'm not a big fan of public speaking, but I did have one question for you if it's all the same to you."

Sully lifted his brow in question. "Go on."

"I was wondering if you have it in you to forgive me for my rash behavior the other day. I don't know what came over me, but I guess I lost it a little and withdrew. The thing is, I enjoy your company, Sully. We don't know each other that well—"

The sound of someone clearing their throat in the silent room caused everyone to turn their heads toward Zoey, who was wearing a sneaky little smirk on her face that Sully knew meant she knew everything that had gone on.

"As I was saying before I was rudely interrupted," Izzy continued, taking a deep breath, "we don't know each other that well, but I'd like to get to know you even better. To quote an oldie but goodie, 'I think this is the beginning of a beautiful friendship.' Sorry, that's my mom's favorite film. So Sullivan Forester, what say we pick up where we left off?"

Sully reached for Izzy's hands and twined his fingers with hers. "I thought you'd never ask." He winked as he leaned down to kiss her and the whole room broke out in applause. Sully raised his hand in the air and waved everyone to work. "You people need to get busy. I'll take care of this." Izzy laughed as he pulled her into his arms.

He grabbed her hand and led her down the hall to his office and pulled her in for a more intimate kiss.

"What changed your mind?"

She pressed her forehead to his. "You did of course."

"Me? What did I do to sway you?"

"It's kind of what you did do and what you didn't do." She swiped her tongue across the tip of his nose. "What you didn't do was press me. You let me figure it out myself. I appreciated you giving me the space I needed."

"Now I'm terribly curious about what I did do to persuade you to come back."

She grinned, one side of her mouth raising a little higher than the other. "You know when I was on my stomach, watching the mama bear and her babies?"

He'd started kissing a trail along her neck as she spoke. "Uh-huh."

"It was such an amazing experience to see them out there in the wild. And you and I were lying there naked in the wild. And to be one with nature like that was such an incredible feeling, and then you did what you did, which was so carnal yet so perfect at that moment in time. We were one with the elements. That. How could I not want at the very least a command performance with you after experiencing that?"

He settled kisses on her throat and beneath her chin as she kept talking.

"Now, I'm not gonna lie," she said. "I was a bit freaked out by that picture going viral. I mean what if that had been us naked?"

"Think how jealous people would be."

"Think how mortified I'd be when my mother found out."

"Or just think of it as someday our children are going to look at that picture and know that was the moment their parents fell in love."

"Why Mr. Forester, don't you think you're jumping the gun a bit suggesting such declarations of possible love?"

Sully stopped kissing her and fixed his emerald eyes on her lapis ones. "Eleanor and Jed hardly knew each other when they decided to stay together for the rest of their lives." He stroked his fingers through her hair as he spoke. "Of course nowadays we don't have to make choices like that—we can take the time to truly get to know everything about each other before we commit for all eternity—while having great sex, I might add. But the thing is, I get it." His eyes softened a little. "I understand how she and Jed made the decision they made. Because I think that's how I feel about you. And if I did have to choose, if I had to marry you or lose you, I know what my decision would be, even without knowing every little detail about you. I'd know we'd have all our lives to learn that. But for now, I am going to savor spending every minute with you and figuring out exactly what makes you tick and what makes you crazy in a good way and even what makes you crazy in a bad way. Making you happy and proving to you that I'm the one for you will give me a great job, Isabelle Strong, so I hope you're willing to stick around for a while longer as we play this thing out."

Izzy pretended to fan herself as she considered his offer.

"Wow. That's a lot to take in. But the thing I liked the most about it was thinking about how one day, our kids are going to see the picture of exactly when we fell in love. It will be a moment we can look forward to." She draped her arms over his neck. "In the meantime, any chance we can act out my cowgirl boot fantasy anytime soon?"

He lifted his brow. "You mean up against the wall, those boots hooked at the ankles, behind me? Gah! I've got a hundred people out there doing my work for me, and now I'm going to be counting the minutes till they all leave—"

She tapped his nose. "It'll let the anticipation build. Something to look forward to."

He shook his head. "If you only knew how badly I want it."

"Not nearly as badly as I do."

Chapter Twenty-Two

SHORTLY after midnight, Sully called everyone to attention.

"Listen up, everyone. I think we've found our winner. And I think you're going to be surprised by it."

He held up an iPad opened to the winning email:

Dear Mr. Forester,

I can' believe what a generous offer you've made to share this ring with someone you think will appreciate it. I'm sure you've received many wonderful replies from all over the world. I'd like to tell you why I'd love to win it: because I'd love to finally make my girlfriend of forty-five years, Alice, an honest woman.

Alice and I have been together since we were young women. Back then you could no sooner be with someone of your own sex than you could have flown to the moon. Well, actually, there were people starting to fly to the moon back then. But the idea of two women loving each other and wanting to spend their lives together was one that society forbade. So for a long time, Alice and I tried to pretend we didn't need each other. Both of us had parents who were trying to get us married off. But neither of us would relent. Years passed and we remained together, technically as roommates, but for all intents and purposes we were married, at least spiritually.

Alice has always been the one for me. But last year Alice was diagnosed with a particularly aggressive form of cancer that she's been fighting with everything she's got. We don't know what the future holds for her. But I do know that after all of these years, I would love to surprise her by making our relationship legal in the eyes of the law and everybody.

I love Alice Finnegan with all my heart. She's a good, kind woman and to be honest, I don't know what I'll do if I lose her. She's been my everything for all of these years, and I'd love to let the world know how much she means to me.
Respectfully,
Sophie Jordan

Izzy handed Sully a tissue to wipe the tears that were filling his eyes.

"We've read amazing letters from so many different people, so many walks of life, but something about Sophie's letter struck a chord in me. So it is with great pleasure that I will be notifying her and announcing on my Facebook page that Sophie Jordan will be the proud new owner of the dreaded ring."

The crowd burst into applause.

"And along with this ring I am handing over to her all of the public attention that has befallen me since I made this announcement. As much as I'm grateful for the attention I was able to garner in seeking the right recipient of the ring, I have to say, if I never see my name in the spotlight again, it'll be too soon. I get to go back to being a normal guy, albeit one who found my very own precious gem in the process of getting rid of another valuable treasure. And while I know that Sophie Jordan considers herself one lucky woman to have found the love of her life, I feel so fortunate that out of nowhere, Izzy Strong decided to grace me with her abundance. Let's all raise our glasses and toast." He held his beer bottle in the air. "To love."

"And now I think Izzy has one last request for the evening: that everyone please get going now because we've got to make up for lost time."

With that everyone clapped and laughed and quickly slipped out the door, leaving them to their own creative devices and maybe to that precision tool Izzy was so happy to get to know.

Thank you so much for reading **_Boy Toy!_** I hope you enjoyed it! If so, please help others find this book:

1. Help other people find this book by writing a review.

2. Sign up for my new releases email so you can find out about the next book as soon as it's available and get fun giveaways.
http://eepurl.com/baaewn

3. Like my Facebook page.
www.facebook.com/jennygardinerbooks

And I love to hear from readers! Let me know what you think about my books! You can write to me at jenny@jennygardiner.net, and visit me on the web at www.jennygardiner.net.

Keep reading for a sample from Cabana Boy – the third book in the **Confessions of a Chick Magnet** series.

Cabana Boy

By

Jenny Gardiner

Chapter One

WHEN Fletcher Campbell first interviewed for the production assistant job with revered film producer Justine Gaynor, he was super excited at the prospect of attending poolside meetings as a perk of the job. After a succession of crap jobs waiting tables while trying to break into the film business, he figured this was merely payoff for his hard work and persistence.

"Everyone out here does them," she'd told him, arms spread wide at the outdoor café where she'd interviewed him. "No reason to waste this sunshine and warm weather!"

Which suited him just fine. After all, he loved being in the outdoors. Having grown up in Montana, the outdoors was practically his middle name. He'd only moved out to L.A. after college to try his hand in the film industry, but he had to admit he greatly missed all that time he used to spend hiking and biking and kayaking and fishing. In L.A. it seemed he devoted most of his time to sitting in traffic sucking in exhaust fumes, which was kind of painful for someone accustomed to the wide open spaces around his hometown of Bristol, Montana, where a hike in nearby Glacier National Park was as likely to yield a grizzly bear sighting as an outing in L.A. would involve a glimpse of a Kardashian or two. He'd take a bear over a Kardashian any day.

But he recognized that this was the cost of pursuing a career he'd gotten hooked on after being hired as an extra in a film that was shot on location in Glacier when he was home for summer break during his freshman year of college. That was a memorable summer not only for his "star turn", as it were, as one of two hundred people in a crowd scene in the park, but also because it was when he and Cricket Ferguson called it quits, after having dated exclusively since the ninth grade. Ugh, but he didn't want to think about that—no matter how much time had passed, it still felt raw to him, so many words left unspoken. But he was in L.A. now, with a new life, big dreams, no need to waste time dwelling on what was. Or could have been.

At today's production meeting, scheduled at his boss's sprawling Beverly Hills mansion, he ended up being the only one in attendance besides his boss, who weirdly insisted on wearing a bikini, even though she was well past the age— and youthful vigor—that one would expect with someone voluntarily exposing so much flesh in a bathing suit. Oh well, he figured if she was happy in it, that's what mattered.

Her pool—one of those sprawling, dark bottomed Gunite types—boasted a waterfall and a bridge which bisected the whole pool, and was so large you needed a bridge to get to the other side, otherwise you'd be exhausted navigating your way around it. He'd never seen something like this in a backyard pool. Clearly he wasn't in Montana any more. She had a wait staff of three who she'd dismissed just as soon as they'd delivered drinks to the two of them. Which was weird—day-drinking during a business meeting? How very Mad Men of her. Good thing he could hang with the best of them after imbibing several drinks.

Fletch tried not to gawk at Justine as she perched, cross-legged, on the overstuffed sofa beneath the shade of a massive umbrella. Man, in the short time he'd been in L.A., he'd never seen so many women so overwrought in an effort to attempt to defy aging, and Justine fit that bill perfectly. First off, bikinis weren't exactly forgiving when it came to hiding what nature hadn't gotten quite right. Or what time had betrayed on a person. So while her surgically-overhauled face was pulled so taut you could probably bounce a quarter off of her cheeks, her neck was encircled with telltale sagging flesh that reminded him of the rings around a tree trunk that told you how old the thing was.

Granted, her arms were a testament to her personal trainer, who was usually leaving the office just as Fletcher was arriving each morning. Whatever that man was doing, he was making sure her guns were tip-top. Same with her long legs, which he knew—because he'd been the one stuck scheduling the expensive appointments—had been CoolSculpted into as cellulite-free an existence as was technologically possible, as was her belly. And she was spray-tanned to within an inch of her life.

But all that work, well, with the right clothing, you could maybe shave off ten years from your age, appearance-wise. But half-naked in a skimpy bikini? It all just looked the opposite of young. Not that he was judging her. He was, however, kind of getting the vibe that she had designs on him, and he wanted to be loud and clear that he had no plans to tangle up any sheets with his boss, even if hers were the gold-karat-threaded, silk jacquard Charlotte Thomas ones, which cost more than his beat-up clunker of a truck did. He should know, because he was tasked with ordering her sheets, natch.

He'd had a fantasized notion of production assistants actually doing something involving something like producing, but if he had to be honest with himself, in the few months since he'd been out here, the only thing he'd done was his demanding boss's bidding, whether that meant chauffeuring her around L.A.—she said it was because he was far more handsome than her regular driver (thank goodness for GPS, since he hardly had committed the geography to memory since arriving here)—or scheduling her weekly Brazilian wax, which he felt bordered on TMI but he was trying to be a cooperative employee so what was he to do?

Speaking of Brazilian wax, her thong bikini bottom was cut high enough on her thigh and down toward her crotch that there was no question she'd made it to her appointment with Brigitte this week to ensure not a stray hair was to be had. Normally it would have turned him on upon getting a teasing glance like that on a woman, big time. After all, he'd helped Cricket do the honors—albeit with a razor—back when they were together. It was the most erotic thing he'd ever done, shaving her there. But with Justine, ugh, he simply mentally shuddered. It would have been like lusting after someone's nana. In fact, she was pretty much old enough to be his grandmother. He closed his eyes against the thought.

"Fletcher, be a dear and help me get some sunscreen on," she said, waving the bottle of suntan lotion at him. "Must fight these damaging UV rays." She winked at him and he winced, steeling himself to just put sunscreen on her back. But he knew that wasn't what she'd planned.

He stood up from his seat and walked to where Justine sat on the sofa, and he wondered where he was supposed to sit while doing this. It would be one thing if she were lying on her stomach. He'd squirt some lotion, politely dab it around, and then beg off when it came to what to do with her exposed butt cheeks. That was hers to figure out. But no. She was sitting there, her legs now extended, her ample fake tits—you could tell they were fake because of the telltale line that ridged her chest where a pouch of saline rested inside of each one—perched so unnaturally high atop her chest. Yuck. It was all so icky. He wondered why women didn't grow old gracefully out here. He thought about how pretty his own mother was, with her salt-and-pepper hair, which she wore in a bob cropped to her shoulder, and the laugh lines that life had given her lighting up her face with joy.

He didn't want to think about his mother's boobs, but he was certain they weren't parked on her chest like a diving board urging all comers to take the plunge. Geeze, he'd take ten aging-gracefully women over one in massive-denial-of-Father-Time version any old day. Of course his mom was a grandma now and he saw how her grandchildren loved to press up against her soft body and snuggle into her loving warmth. Besides, every man knew that a little meat on the bones was an added bonus. Skin and bones ladies like Justine, with her hips jutting out like mountain peaks, and her zero percent body fat, was just a bit extreme; they just didn't appeal to him.

He took a deep breath. He almost wanted to plug his nose, as if his mom was forcing the five-year-old version of him to down a forkful of stinky cauliflower. *Okay, Fletch. You can do this.* Unpleasant work have-to's were part and parcel to climbing the ladder in Hollywood. Not that he would succumb to a little slap-and-tickle with the woman to get his way—no way, no how—but capitulating when your boss coerces you into applying sunscreen didn't seem too far out of the ordinary.

"Uh, er, where did you want this?" he squirted some of the sunscreen into his hand, then leaned over her, figuring he'd go for the arms, which seemed a safe bet. How much trouble could he get into there? He stared at her wrist—far, far from even a hint of any erogenous zones (although didn't Cricket love it when he stroked her wrist with his thumb?)—

and began massaging in the lotion.

Justine let out a tiny moan.

Shit. Was this turning on this biddy? He accelerated the application pace, moving his palms up her forearms, speed-slathering toward her bicep, hoping to the good lord above that he could be done with this and get down to business. Of course he knew he'd have to lean over get the other arm, so he sucked it up and did it, gnawing on his cheek the whole time. When done with arm number two, he placed the bottle on the sofa next to her, hoping to return to his own seat, a safe several feet away.

But instead she pointed the toes on her right foot and extended her leg and foot toward his thigh, dragging her gelled toenails (he should know: he made the appointment) up his thigh till he thought he might scream.

Fletcher never thought the idea of a woman dragging a toe up his leg toward his dick would be a turn-off, but damn, when a granny-substitute—and a bad one at that—was doing it, boy was it ever.

"You forgot these," Justine said, flexing and pointing her foot, as if that provocative move had any effect on him. Christ, what could he say? If he told her that was inappropriate, she'd fire him on the spot. If he proceeded on demand, well, then his hands would be sliding up her muscled thighs, eventually practically smoothing over her pudenda.

Ha! He hadn't thought of that term since the test on female anatomy in his middle school sex-ed class. He could still picture an awkward Mrs. Morrison with her pointer stick aiming at the illustration of the female anatomy on the board and cringed at the thought. He sure as hell couldn't mentally refer this woman's thing as a pussy. If he did, he'd never think of a pussy the same again. Although he sure as hell wanted to think of a pussy, any pussy, simply to purge what he was doing from his mind. So he pretended he was slicking the sunscreen along Cricket's thighs, strong and sturdy from a lifetime or riding and living an outdoor life of hiking and running and biking.

He closed his eyes. *Remind me again why I left Cricket for this?* He squirted some more lotion in his hands and raced his fingers along her legs and thighs, rapidly doing what he had to, just to get the chore over with. Now he really understood that phrase, *lie back and think of England.*

Justine moaned again and suddenly ground her hips toward his hand, causing his fingertips to slip dangerously close to the thigh-edge of her bikini. For a second almost threw up in his mouth. He was certain that real nanas didn't force guys young enough to be their grandsons to finger their twats. He pulled his hands away as if he'd touched a hot stove, and dusted them off, as if to segue to more important business.

"Okay. Well, then, weren't we here to brainstorm about the release of Icicle Man?"

This was Justine's latest film, something to do with some dude who froze to death in the mountains while searching for some elusive clues to his own past. Right about now Fletcher was putting his current fate up there with Icicle Man in the sucky outcomes department. Freezing to death almost sounded preferable to his own.

Just then Justine reached out her hand and pressed her palm to the crotch on the outside of his Chubbies trunks—the ones with the silverback gorillas all over them. If only he had the strength of a silverback, he'd knock her out of the way and run, far from this whacked-out woman. He tried to stick his butt out, away from her, removing proximity so she couldn't grab his nuts next.

"Oh, have some fun," Justine said, dragging her Shellacked sanguine-red nails along his thigh, making the hair stand on end. And not in a good way. He could feel his balls shriveling.

He had to think quickly, or this would only deteriorate into something even worse.

"It's just that my girlfriend—"

She lifted an eyebrow. "Girlfriend?" She waggled an admonishing finger. "And here I thought you were unencumbered." She thrust out her lower lip in a pout like she was a 'tween told she had an eleven o'clock curfew.

He sucked so badly at lying, especially thinking on his feet like this. "Well, my girlfriend from back home, we decided to give it another go. And, well, I'm about to ask her to marry me."

Justine looked up. "Marriage? How very provincial," she said. "Is that what they do wherever you're from?"

He squinted at her. "You mean get married?"

She nodded, once again dragging her daggers up his thigh, which made his abdomen contract from the chill it induced. "Aren't you too young for such adult things?"

Now that pissed him off. Too young to get married but not too young for a cougar thrice his age to come onto him like he was a slab of raw beef thrown at her? Yeah, right.

"I'm plenty old enough, thanks," he said, wiping the spare sunscreen off on his trunks as he delicately stepped back away from her.

"Where is this place you're from, where your girlfriend pines away for you?" she said it in such a way that she clearly felt his life was some sort of amusement for her to play with, a cat with a ball of yarn.

"I'm—we're—from Montana."

She turned her head upward toward him. "Oh, really?

One of those places with snow-capped mountains?"

He nodded and knit his brow, not knowing where she was headed with this. "Why do you ask?"

She held up her pointer finger. "Eureka, I think we've just found where we're going to premier our film!" she started to laugh. "We're going to Wherever-You're-From, Montana, and maybe then I can even have a word with that fiancé-girlfriend of yours."

Fletch's face fell. Shit. Fiancé-girlfriend. How was he going to get out of this—bringing his horny boss back home to size up what she saw as competition from a non-existent now-former girlfriend (and never fiancé) who could give a half a shit about anything to do with Fletcher Campbell at this point and would assuredly never cover for his lies.

To think he thought he'd been making progress professionally. *Sonofabitch.*

Chapter Two

CRICKET Ferguson had just finished mucking the stalls in the barn and decided to take a few minutes to enjoy the late-day sun as it painted a soothing, melon-hued light across the fields. Today was one of those days that reminded her why she wanted to spend the rest of her life in this amazing little hamlet she called home.

First she'd risen well before dawn, roused her Australian Shepherd Dingo for a four-mile run, a practice that cleared her mind and helped her plan her day. After returning home for a quick shower, she slipped down a flight of stairs to the patisserie she'd opened a year ago, and got to work on the array of pastries and café food she'd planned to offer the good folks of Bristol today.

She and her assistant, Darby Cunningham had such fun working side-by-side it was a wonder that what she did was considered a job. After a couple of years of working for a succession of imperious pastry chefs, it took coming home and opening Patisserie Cricket to really feel like what she was doing was what she was meant to be doing. Yeah, yeah, Patisserie Cricket was hardly the most French of names. But she decided that she needed to name her shop something as no-nonsense and basic as she was. Besides, this was Montana: not like anyone out here would be flocking to a shop with some hoity-toity French name. Here in Montana, folks wanted things more simple, and she was happy to offer that.

After spending the day creating and baking, she'd headed over to her parents' ranch for a late-afternoon ride with her horse, Bunny, with Dingo running loops around them as they rode out past the hay fields and meadows and into the lush forest surrounding the farm. Riding in the woods during these autumn afternoons took her breath away, with the breathtaking palette of colors Mother Nature showed off, as leaves prepared to fall in anticipation of the first snowfall. This was God's country, so beautiful it took your breath away, and she loved every moment she could take in the splendor of it. Despite her time in the cosmopolitan city of Paris while she trained, and then briefly on the East Coast afterwards to get experience under her belt, this was the place that called to her. Sure, she'd needed to get away for a while after Fletch bailed on her. But now she'd wrestled with those demons, carved out a new life for herself, and at last, everything was falling into place.

While she leaned against the split-rail fence, her cowboy hat cocked on her head, gnawing on a piece of straw, looking out on the horizon, her phone dinged. She pulled it out to find a most unexpected email. It was from a big L.A. production company, wanting to place an order for an obscene amount of food for a film premier that was going to happen right here in little ol' Bristol, which could be a fantastic boon for her business. She'd talk to Darby first thing in the morning to plot out a strategy to handle this order before she replied to it in details. While her business had been doing quite well, this could put her on the map— not that she was looking to be put on a map. But still, anything like this could get word of mouth about her baking skills going beyond the borders of Bristol, and you never knew how that could benefit her fledgling patisserie.

After returning to Bristol last year, Cricket had been stuck for while living at home, far past the point at which she'd hoped to be under her parents' roof. Finally this past summer, she and her dad had taken a sledgehammer to the room above the pastry shop, and then got to work creating a cozy apartment she could call her own. It made her heart sing each night when she went upstairs to her very own space. It was all she needed in life and she was finally feeling content.

Which had taken a while, since Fletcher Campbell had crushed her hopes and dreams by blowing out of Bristol in pursuit of some pie-in-the-sky dreams of Hollywood fame and fortune. For the life of her she didn't understand it, but she also couldn't stop it. Even though they'd talked for years about their future together—they'd even named their kids!—all of a sudden, poof, he was gone, leaving not a trace behind.

It had hurt at the time, and was part of the reason she took off for Paris to learn to bake, but she learned the hard way that with pain, comes growth, and finally she was starting to feel that she'd gotten over him, and practically grown ten feet tall in the process. And now she was perfectly content not to have any man getting in the way of her happiness. She had her shop, her apartment, and Dingo, so life was full.

As Cricket read the email, she wondered for a moment if she was picking up some snark in between the lines.

"*Cricket,*" it said. "*What a charming name. One of those names the boys probably love to bits.*"

Whatever the hell that meant. What a weird comment for someone to make in a professional context.

"*But I bet you don't even think about that, what with your fiancé and all. I'll look forward to sitting down with you and finding out everything about you.*"

Cricket squinted. Fiance? Huh? And why would she have any reason to find anything out about her? Maybe she was talking about her menu options? Or how she planned to serve it all at the film opening?

She shook her head. If there was one thing she'd learned

since leaving Bristol for a while, it was that people were strange. Plenty were nice and normal and all that, but there were some weirdos out there, and she was just going to chalk the comments up to that. After all, those rich Hollywood types would no doubt be more likely to be a little eccentric than your average Bristoller. Or was it Bristollian? She never did get that right.

Cricket thought about her name, which she always kind of liked, even though she never really wanted to think about the genesis of it. The story was, she was conceived in a hayfield, with crickets trumpeting their horny mating call to the accompaniment of her folks doing the same damned thing. A fact that always made her roll her eyes. It's one thing if you're the one doing it in the hayfield, but your parents? Please. That is so need-to-know basis. Nevertheless, she always thought the name Cricket had a nice ring to it.

Well, she'd just dismiss the weird line of questioning about her name. And the fiancé thing, that woman—Cricket glanced down at her phone to see: Justine Gaynor. Well, then, Justine Gaynor, she must have had that information flat-out wrong. She wondered why she surmised that, but then just figured it wasn't relevant. As long as she got this kick-ass order in and could fulfill it, the woman could call her The Queen of England.

She gave a whistle for Dingo and hopped into her truck, securing her dog into her seatbelt before fastening her own. She had a huge event to plan for, so she wanted to get home to her mystery fiancé and get started on it, she thought with a laugh.

Cabana Boy

Coming January 8, 2019

About the Author

Jenny Gardiner is the author of #1 Kindle Bestseller *Slim to None* and the award-winning novel *Sleeping with Ward Cleaver*. Her latest works are the *It's Reigning Men* series, the *Royal Romeos* series, the *Falling for Mr. Wrong* series and her new *Confessions of a Chick Magnet* series. She also published the memoir *Winging It: A Memoir of Caring for a Vengeful Parrot Who's Determined to Kill Me,* now re-titled *Bite Me: a Parrot, a Family and a Whole Lot of Flesh Wounds*; the novels *Anywhere but Here*; *Where the Heart Is*; the essay collection *Naked Man on Main Street*, and *Accidentally on Purpose* and *Compromising Positions* (writing as Erin Delany); and is a contributor to the humorous dog anthology *I'm Not the Biggest Bitch in This Relationship*.

Her work has been found in Ladies Home Journal, the Washington Post, Marie-Claire.com, and on NPR's Day to Day. She was also a columnist for Charlottesville's Daily Progress for over a decade, and is the Volunteer Coordinator for the Virginia Film Festival.

She has worked as a professional photographer, an orthodontic assistant (learning quite readily that she was not cut out for a career in polyester), a waitress (probably her highest-paying job), a TV reporter, a pre-obituary writer, as well as a publicist to a United States Senator (where she first learned to write fiction). She's photographed Prince Charles (and her assistant husband got him to chuckle!), Elizabeth Taylor, and the president of Uganda. She and her family and menagerie of pets now live a less exotic life in Virginia.

Visit Jenny at her website and sign up for her <u>newsletter</u>, her <u>blog</u>, or find her on <u>Facebook</u> and <u>Twitter</u>. And every blue moon she'll post adorable pictures of her pets on <u>Instagram</u> as @thejennygardiner.